Th

M000158786

The Novel

by Nawal El Saadawi

translated by Omnia Amin & Rick London

Interlink Books

An imprint of Interlink Publishing Group, Inc.
Northampton, Massachusetts

First published in 2009 by

INTERLINK BOOKS
An imprint of Interlink Publishing Group, Inc.
46 Crosby Street, Northampton, MA 01060
www.interlinkbooks.com

Library of Congress Cataloging-in-Publication Data
Sa'dawi, Nawal.
[Riwayah. English]
The novel / Nawal El Saadawi ; translated from the Arabic by Omnia
Amin and Rick London. -- 1st American ed.
p. cm.
ISBN 978-1-56656-732-9 (pbk.)
I. Amin, Umniyah. II. London, Rick. III. Title.
PJ7862.A3R5913 2008
892.7'36--dc22
2008015957

Printed and bound in the United States of America

To request our complete 40-page full-color catalog,
please call us toll free at 1-800-238-LINK, visit our
website at www.interlinkbooks.com, or write to
Interlink Publishing
46 Crosby Street, Northampton, MA 01060
e-mail: info@interlinkbooks.com

To migrating birds,
escaping death…
To male and female wanderers,
in search of hope.

The novel caused tremendous outrage.

The young woman was twenty-three years old. Her father, unknown. She had no family, no university degree, no national identity card. Her life became her first novel. She wrote it out with a pen, without being a recognized writer, without having first read the great words of prophets and poets and famous writers. Her name did not appear on the lists of prominent female authors.

Her frame was sinewy and slender, as she constantly pursued her daily bread. But her backbone was solid. Her facial features were sharpened by excessive thinness, etched in bone as enduring as stone.

Elections were approaching, and the season was dominated by sex scandals and by reports of the corruption of both male and female nominees (of which men were undoubtedly the majority).

1

The protagonist in the novel was a member of the Shura Council, the upper body of Parliament. At fifty-four, he was the youngest candidate. He seemed to be an athletic man; he played golf every day; he had a long, brisk stride. He had a tan, a close shave, and a gleam in his eye. His suit was elegant and his tie colorful. He smelled of lavender aftershave. He worked for a large daily newspaper. He had published eight novels and was at work on his ninth. His name was Roustum.

~※~

Roustum used to walk by the Nile on warm, moonlit nights. He would stop by the riverside at a kiosk called The Boutique. It was owned by the son of one of the martyrs of war. He wore a long white gown and had a long black beard. Prayer beads hung at the front of the shop, where the proprietor displayed golden-covered Qurans, incense burners, Ramadan calendars, and veils for women.

He beamed, as usual, when he saw Roustum approach.

"Hello, Pasha."

The young man handed him a small piece of the substance one puts in the hookah, or under the tongue, and a novel covered in thick wrapping paper that did not reveal the book's title, along with a calendar for Ramadan. The Ramadan month was approaching, along with the elections.

"What's the news, Mohammed?"

Roustum had a manly voice, coarse and gruff, full of masculinity and thick smoke. It was attractive to the young women who read his popular novels.

"The dollar is rising, Pasha, and the Egyptian pound is falling."

Roustum handed him a brown envelope with an eagle's head printed on it, wrapped in heavy plastic tape. The young man carried it in both hands with great care, as if it were a bird about to flap its wings and fly. He disappeared into a wooden vault inside The Boutique and after a few minutes returned, carrying a small black plastic bag.

"Count them, Pasha."

"You want me to count them again after you, Mohammed?"

"How many Ramadan calendars do you want?"

"As many as there are voters—two, three, or four thousand."

"All the people support you and God is with you."

"God is above everyone."

❧

At night before going to sleep, Roustum tore the thick cover off the novel as if he were tearing the clothes off of a woman's body. He loved reading while smoking and drinking. His desire, like that of every other man and woman, was aroused by the forbidden. Everything forbidden is desirable, as they say.

The photo of the young author was printed on the back, a small square. His eyes fixed on her features. They were prominent and stony, and her eyes stared back at him, piercing, cutting into him like a sharp knife. She was twenty-three—thirty-one years younger than he. She was born in the spring of 1981, the year he published his second novel, which won the highest award. He'd received his prize from the president himself, five months before his assassination.

The young woman's face started to appear in his dreams.

⁓

The young woman ran off to a faraway place to write the novel.

She took with her only a single suitcase containing her clothes and her papers, and the child she carried inside her. She traveled to a distant shore to be closer to the sea. She was seeking to escape the dark walls, arrest, the death sentence. She wanted to give life to her child, the fruit of a sacred love, of divine semen in the womb of a virgin.

At night, when the wind was silent and the sea asleep, the unborn child slept in her depths, its father unknown. She knew neither the novel's nor the child's name.

4

People lived in fear. What frightened them most was the unknown: things that were nameless. The devil they knew by name. And also the names of the gods.

The young woman switched off the light near her bed and returned in her memory to her hometown. She'd crossed the sea from the south to the north to get away from it. Vision needed distance, away from noise and loud shouting, away from the dust of the alley and blazing summer heat. She unwrapped her mind. She exposed her face to the sunlight. She swam in the sea like a silver fish and opened her eyes to a limitless horizon.

A buzzing in her ears reminded her of the flies in the neighborhood of al-Sayyida Zaynab, the ticking of the old clock near her pillow, the supplications of the beggars in front of the mosque as they asked vainly for mercy and justice from heaven.

Heaven arched overhead in eternal silence, except for the few rare moments in winter when it asserted a vow of thunder and a faint drizzle fell and dried up.

༺❀༻

They sat sipping wine in a small coffee shop near al-Tahrir Square. After the first glass a sad intoxication overtook her. Samih sat beside her in a gray suit without a tie. His face was pale and slender and his eyes green. Carmen sat in front of her in a colorful dress. Her brown, thick hair tossed as she moved her head with uninhibited laughter. Beside her, Roustum with his tan, in a sky-blue suit and a red tie with blue dots. His eyes wandered away as he filled their empty cups. He handed her a cup. Their eyes met in a quick glance, then his eyes wandered off once more. Even when she was absent, her eyes gazed at him, fixed, piercing, cutting like a sharp knife. Two big eyes, dark blue like the ocean, in which colors and races have melted together, their depth a lure beyond sex.

~✾~

The city of Cairo is feminine at night. By day its conscious mind believes in a masculine god. The feminine presides in its unconscious.

She used to wander its streets by foot or with Roustum in his Mercedes, which was the same color as his suit. The first time he invited her alone, Carmen was in New York participating in a conference on the postmodern novel. Samih was in Assiut giving a lecture at the university on the biology of culture.

On al-Haram Street her eyes fixed on the top of the pyramids. She glanced at Roustum, with his proud nose, his thick African lips, and his arms thick with hair tinted blond by the sun. He moved them with confidence over the steering wheel.

It was the first time he had invited her alone. They were used to being together, the four of them. Something mysterious was happening between them, a flow of ambiguous feelings that caused her anxiety.

When the young woman was alone, a strong feeling of sadness swept over her. The walls of the tiny flat in the cul-de-sac surrounded her. She shared the flat with Gamalat, a middle-aged journalist who was defined by her body. She dyed her hair red with henna and covered it with a white scarf. Her white, plump face was heavily made-up. She outlined her eyes with kohl and darkened her thin eyebrows with eyeliner into a bow shape. She painted her faint lips red.

The flat had two bedrooms, one for the young woman and the other for Gamalat. In each room there was a wide bed made out of dingy wood, an old dresser, and a small table for eating and writing and striking with one's fist in anger. The hall was narrow and dark. One window looked out on the backyard. The kitchen was even darker and only big enough for washing the dishes or standing in front of the stove.

As Roustum drove the car, he said that Cairo crushes the weak. In it, corruption hides beneath the robes of legislation and its ruler wears the white gown of the paternal god. She felt guilty. Why had she accepted his invitation? She was looking for a job, just like the rest of the unemployed men and women whose only hope is to emigrate. The word *homeland* caught in her throat, choking her.

Carmen used to take her out in her Fiat when her husband traveled. She never drove his big Mercedes. She would get her small Fiat out of the garage at their home in Garden City and cross Kasr al-Aini Street to al-Mobtadayan Street. She would enter the blocked alley in the neighborhood of al-Sayyida Zaynab and stop in front of the grim wooden door.

She beeped the horn once or twice and the young woman descended the dark stairs, avoiding the broken step on the ground floor. She rode next to her as they set out for Sahary City. Carmen parked the car in front of the small house in the middle of the desert. They took off their shoes and walked on the soft sand. Carmen told her about a novel she had read or a joke she had heard or something that had happened to her.

Suddenly, she stopped talking. The sound of the desert's silence was pierced as though by a whistle. She had feared the dark since childhood. From a distance, the sand dunes seemed like ghosts. Carmen stood resolutely, gazing toward the top of the distant pyramids.

Carmen's voice reached her, faintly.

"Roustum loves you."

"Your husband?"

"Yes."

Though days passed, Carmen's voice remained in her ears: *Roustum loves you*, the shiver and the surprise shuddering and trembling beneath her ribs—how had Carmen known what she herself did not?

"I know nothing, I swear to God."

"No need to swear to it, I believe you."

In her room in the alley of al-Sayyida she thought of how she had uttered the words, *I swear to God*. It was not her habit to swear to God. She did not respect those who swear to God. They must be liars or they would not need to swear.

Roustum returned from his travels. She heard his voice over the telephone inviting her to a seminar on the novel *Wide Sargasso Sea* by the Caribbean writer Jean Rhys. She liked attending such seminars. They took place at Dar al-Nashr, in Heliopolis, the place Samih had inherited from his father. He had turned it into a center for literature and art.

Once Samih had almost filled her life. The sparkle and the consuming desire of their love had subsided and become like a quiet river, nothing quickening under the ribs, nothing exciting the imagination.

On a distant shore lies the other city. Its name is Barcelona. In the spring its streets are filled with the young, with lithe and slender bodies whose sex cannot be discerned from outer appearances, nothing distinguishing femininity from masculinity except something deep and unconscious. Barcelona is a feminine city, in name and body. The shadow of its mind is masculine. It believes in God the father and his male son, who is carried on the breast of his virgin mother. Its being is subsumed by the name of the Holy Spirit.

❧

Carmen was unable to rid herself of her belief in Christ. Her husband Roustum had never believed in a heavenly god. Philosophy helped him in this. Samih had realized this truth as a child, even before he started school.

The young woman felt inferior. She had never gone to college. She had grown up in poverty and needed to work. She viewed the universe as something that has been eternally and will be forever. She had not concerned herself with how it came to be. She never read religious books. She preferred novels and poetry. Her mind rushed out to the wide horizon while her soul remained imprisoned by her body. The conversations between Samih, Roustum, and Carmen gripped her. She could take part with a cold heart that was free of faith. Yet her guts shivered whenever one of them uttered a blasphemous word.

That was in the early days of their relationship, before she found out that he loved her, even before

Carmen found out. The first to know was Samih. They were sitting, as they usually did, in a small café slowly sipping wine. Samih was speaking about the philosophy of biology and the chemistry of emotions.

After Roustum and Carmen left, she and Samih walked on Kasr al-Nile Bridge. The waves on the surface shone under the light like silver fish.

"Have you noticed anything about Roustum?" Samih asked, holding her hand.

"What do you mean?"

"I think he loves you."

The bridge shook under her feet. She stopped. How had Samih noticed what she had not, though it was about her?

~✤~

The young woman looked out from her high window toward the port of Barcelona. She followed the water of the Mediterranean to the south and then east, to the shore of Alexandria. No matter how far she traveled a longing remained. She had no country, no place of birth. She had no family. She had no childhood, no tales of jinn and ghouls. She sometimes yearned for the smell of the land, the pavement, the sewers. The smell crossed the sea. Time eased the decrepitude of the past.

The young woman lived in a small room on the roof of a high building. The building belonged to a woman called Yolanda who lived on the first floor. She had a liquor shop on the ground floor, overlooking the main square, and a small restaurant famous for its *paella marinara*, a mixture of fish, tomatoes, onions, garlic, and yellow rice that shone in the light, steaming. It stirred her appetite whenever she passed the restaurant. The price for this meal was nine euros. She had no work or source of income.

Yolanda was short and fat. Gray rings circled her eyes and her face was pale and flabby. She tied back her blond hair with a black ribbon. Her children were scattered all over the world, except for her son Francisco, who impersonated Salvador Dali in the Ramblas. He stood like a statue, with an enormous mustache and his body painted white. He pantomimed, then froze again. People passed and looked at him with an admiration that was not without pity. Sometimes one might throw a coin in the hat at his feet.

The first time she saw Yolanda she was sitting in the restaurant eating *paella marinara*. She saw her gazing at the shrimp and the golden rice vaporous with steam. Yolanda proposed an arrangement and, out of necessity, she accepted. She would work four days a week in the restaurant in exchange for a room on the roof.

"But where shall I eat, Yolanda?" She spoke in deficient Catalan while pointing to her mouth with her hand.

Yolanda nodded toward the back room of the restaurant. She looked at her thin body and pale face.

"I don't think you eat very much, my daughter."

She spoke the word *daughter* in a motherly voice, which her cruel demeanor hadn't suggested, or her metallic voice, which clicked like an adding machine. She offered her a plate of hot paella. The young woman worked until midnight that very day. Then she took the elevator to the top floor and climbed the stairs to the roof. She paused for a while to smell the sea and to look out on the port of Barcelona in the distance, the ships on the shore, the statue of Christopher Columbus with his hand raised, pointing a finger toward the sea and to the south, to the north of Africa.

Francisco came to her one night and stood beside her on the roof, smelling the air. He began to teach her Catalan and she taught him Arabic. He said that Christopher Columbus was pointing in the wrong direction—he had traveled west to America and not south to Africa. He held her hand and looked into her eyes under the light of the moon. His eyes were blue and shining, but they became dark at night, resembling Roustum's eyes, and sometimes Samih's.

✿

She crossed the sea in her sleep to return to her bedroom in the cul-de-sac of al-Sayyida Zaynab. It resembled her bedroom in Barcelona. The gloomy walls suffocated her soul and the old wooden bed moaned under the two bodies colliding in the dark.

13

She recognized one of them: her own. She'd carried this body wherever she'd gone. She knew it quite well. She caressed it with her fingertips, with an old longing. She felt estranged from it for a brief moment, as if her body belonged to another woman, but then she recognized it once more: her thin brown fingers, her nails cut short according to Yolanda's instructions, and the weak shiver that came from the mysterious sadness inside her.

She barely knew the other body. His love-making was a pantomime. He whispered what maybe sounded like her name in her ear and she answered without knowing his. She called him Francisco or Roustum or Samih.

Although she was a liberal person, a woman was trapped inside her. Her mind and body were outside the confines of this prison but part of her remained locked up. Was it her spirit that was unable to break free? The word *spirit* is feminine in the language of the Quran, and, despite that, refers to the god of the sky.

Roustum used to say that language preceded religion. "And Eve is the origin of existence. Adam is no more than a branch."

Then he would look at her with a gleam in his eyes. He studied the effect of his words on her. His wife Carmen clapped her soft hands like a child in admiration.

14

"Bravo! You are the most beautiful man in the world, Roustum."

He slid a quick look at her. Their eyes met for an instant and moved away. She was overcome by mysterious feelings, some sad and others happy. His big hazel eyes showed a mixture of blood from the north and south, the chemistry of the east and west. He had studied philosophy at Cambridge, then quit to write a novel. Life's peculiarities were at the crux of his dual personality. His lips were filled with abundant desire. But the cold, neutral look in his eyes spoke of fate and destiny.

Samih was different. His green eyes were warm, and his lips thin and cold. His mother had been a dancer in an amusement park in Alexandria. She'd adored the old Egyptian art. After she danced, she did not give her body to the men: she joined them in conversation about art and philosophy until dawn. An army officer who owned a printing press fell in love with her. He was killed by a bomb during the 1956 tripartite invasion of Port Said, when Samih was only three months old. His mother continued with her career as a dancer until Samih graduated from the University of Alexandria. She sent him to Paris, where he studied tribal cultures and got a Ph.D. in anthropology. His deep yearning for the arts resembled his yearning for his mother. He'd inherited from her a flat overlooking the sea in Alexandria and a flat on the Nile in Garden City. He inherited the printing press in Heliopolis from his father.

Carmen sometimes left her Fiat in the garage. She didn't like to drive in Cairo in the morning. She preferred taking the metro from Saad Zaghloul to the zoo in Giza. She was writing a novel about a veterinarian.

It was a warm day in April. She wore a summer dress that revealed her arms and part of her cleavage. Her dark brown hair fell to her shoulders. On the metro a woman sat opposite her wearing black from head to toe. She could only see two black eyes filled with anger.

Suddenly the woman took a big black scarf from her handbag. She rushed toward Carmen, throwing the scarf over her hair and neck as she screamed, "Wearing the veil is a duty, like prayer!"

Carmen went rigid with fear, and then took the scarf off her head and threw it back at the woman. Then Carmen yanked off the woman's veil and her bald head was uncovered in front of the people on the train.

Roustum laughed when he heard the story.

Samih looked silent and troubled, and then said, "In politics, playing with religion is like playing with fire. Cairo is living on top of a hidden volcano."

Carmen glanced at the news headlines.

SOME MEMBERS OF THE SHURA COUNCIL IN FAVOR OF FORBIDDING ALCOHOL, STONING, WHIPPING, AND CUTTING OFF THE HANDS OF THIEVES

FOURTEEN YOUNG IMMIGRANTS DROWN NEAR THE
SHORE OF BARCELONA

YOUNG WOMAN BROUGHT TO TRIAL: ILLEGITIMATELY
PREGNANT, LACKS MOTHERLY FEELINGS, KILLS CHILD

PEOPLE WITHOUT MANNERS IN THIS AGE OF
DEMOCRACY AND REFORM

Roustum glanced at her. They looked at each other with half-closed eyes, accusing one another in silence. At night they silently embraced. The wife had a sense of smell stronger than a dog's. She knew the scent of other women, especially that of the young woman: the cheap soap, the cheap shampoo, the sweat, and the dust of the cul-de-sac in al-Sayyida.

⁘

The sun shone in Barcelona. Bodies stretched out on the shore under the rays of the golden sun. The young woman wore a white bikini and swam like a silver fish underwater. The seawater was warm in spring. She had forgotten her previous life. Faces were erased from her memory, except for that of the judge as he banged the table with a gavel.

Everything blooms in Barcelona during springtime: the eyes of kittens, the virgins of the east, migrating birds. The sky is transparent blue. One single cloud hid the unsleeping eyes that watched how the young woman behaved. Nothing matched them, except the eyes of Satan, which also hid behind the cloud.

The young woman watched the cloud crawl. It carefully approached the head of Christopher Columbus. On the Ramblas, the young woman walked by flower shops. She waved her arms in acrobatic movements and danced to the music played by a group of young men. She flew in the air like a bird then bent to the ground like a lump of dough. Men and women sat in cafés sipping wine and cold beer. Their eyes shone in the sunlight. They ate leisurely from plates brimming with barbecued fish and clams.

The young woman wore a light summer shirt, a pair of wide black pants, and sneakers. She raced with the wind from Catalonia Square to Port Olympic. The smell of the seaweed and salt took her back to the seashore at Sidi Bishr. She used to swim there with Samih. He swam ahead of her to the rock at Miami. She loved him more in the sea than anywhere else. She had never known the sea in her own childhood. Her mother gave birth to her within black walls. She was born on a strip of pavement.

After dinner the four of them—Roustum, Carmen, Samih, and she—took a walk on Nile Street. They passed a hooker who was leaning her thin body against a lamppost. Her kohl-lined eyes were wide enough to hold the sadness of the whole universe. Roustum and Samih looked her over from head to toe, with a mixture of pity and desire.

"Men have been attracted to hookers from the time of the god Amun, to the times of Moses, Jesus, and Mohammed," Carmen said.

The name *Mohammed* rang in her ears and her body jolted in fear. She was unable to rid herself of her childhood fear of bodies burning in hell.

The alleys of Barcelona reminded her of the alleys of Cairo: the lamps hanging on the doors of ancient houses, the faint light coming from small shops clustered under stone pillars looked like those of Mohammed Ali Street. The shadows of men running in the dark, hookers in high heels and painted faces, their kohl-darkened eyes appearing red, one of them humming an unknown song, one that belongs to every language in the world.

༺

She did not stop seeing Roustum for very long. Carmen came to visit her in her room in al-Sayyida. Gamalat opened the door for her. The young woman was in her room with a headache. She swallowed two kinds of pills: one for contraception and another for depression. Gamalat took out a bottle from a box she kept under her bed. As she sipped wine and ate peanuts, Carmen spoke.

"I don't possess Roustum and he doesn't possess me."

Gamalat interrupted, "Only God possesses us all, Carmen!"

The word *God* rang in her ears, in Gamalat's sharp voice. She bumped the wine bottle, making it wobble on the table. Then she regained her balance. Carmen smiled slightly.

"Roustum is a free man in charge of himself. I can't stop him. Love happens in spite of us—this is at once its pleasure and its pain."

"Carmen, you are quite right!" Gamalat shouted, having become intoxicated with wine.

After Carmen left and the wine wore off, Gamalat said, "Carmen might kill you, my dear. There is no woman in the world who is not jealous over her husband. God has created us out of flesh and blood. We eat, drink, love, hate, and die of jealousy, and we even kill. God has placed the human being above the angels. He has burdened us with fighting the evils inside our selves. This is what we are entrusted to carry, while mountains cannot. What about going out to the movies tonight? There's a great film called *The Fire of Love*. Come on, get out of bed, let's have a bit of fun before we die and go to hell."

※

Gamalat sat next to her in the dark. In the film, an old man falls in love with a young maid. Love dominates his heart and his mind. His wife threatens him. He divorces her and marries the maid, who flees from him at night. She is afraid to go back to her people in the village. She gets rid of the child in her womb and becomes a dancer in one of the nightclubs until she is arrested.

The young woman heard Gamalat's beating heart and heavy breath as she watched the love scenes. She pressed the young woman's hand and her body trembled as the maid was raped in the kitchen. Her faint sighs were barely audible. She wiped away her tears in the dark. After the film was over and the lights switched back on, she saw that Gamalat's eyes were blood red. Gamalat turned her face away and adjusted her veil. She remained silent and gloomy until they got home.

Under her bed the prayer rug was rolled up into a cylinder. Beside it lay a cardboard box. Only one bottle was left inside it. She pulled it out and placed it on top of the table. She bent down once more and pulled the prayer rug from under the bed and rolled it out on the floor. She went to the bathroom for her ablution. After praying, she remained kneeling with her two palms facing up toward the ceiling. She asked God for forgiveness.

Gamalat knew a couple of verses from Omar Khayyam. She chanted them in a trembling voice. She sang out a poem by Abu Nawwas and remembered her late husband. She called him the hell-bound; she was certain that God would throw him into the deepest pit of hell. He had been one of the famous proponents of Islam. He had a heart attack during a meeting with the president. After his death, she discovered that he was married to another woman, with whom he had three sons. He left most of his property to them, and she inherited only the old house in al-Sayyida.

＊

When Roustum entered the young woman's life she seemed to have a settled existence with Samih. Yet her life was a theater of considerable turmoil. She was like a straw blown about by the wind. A young woman without family, money, or beauty. Gamalat looked her over from head to toe, then pursed her lips and clapped her hands together.

"What does whatshisname love about you? You're dark like a barbarian, and you're a bag of bones. God works in mysterious ways!"

Gamalat saw herself as beautiful, with her white skin and plump body, thin lips and round thighs. She listed the phone numbers of her admirers in alphabetical order: Ahmad Ahmad Osama, followed by Bahaa Bahy al-Din Boram.

Her poet friend Miriam, who was placed under the letter M, used to invite Gamalat and the young woman to a boat on the Nile on summer nights. The three of them used to sit next to the water around a table with a pure white tablecloth. The waiter placed bottles of beer before them. Gamalat and Miriam preferred beer to wine during the summer. Miriam hummed her poetry as she sipped the cold beer.

We drink beer because we are thirsty,
but we drink wine because we love it.

Her dark eyes shone. Her skin was the reddish brown of clay and her hair was dark like the night. As she recited her poetry her voice flowed as calmly as the waves of the Nile.

Summer nights in Cairo are wrapped in a sort of magic, with the warm Nile breeze and the moon veiled by a transparent cloud. Water drops shone on crystal glasses as they slowly sipped the cold beer, their rapture made by hot and cold, the ecstasy of drinking in thirst. The young woman stretched her legs on the boat's wooden railing and listened to Miriam sing poetry. A child selling jasmine necklaces approached. He had a long face stained with gray spots and a white circle around his left eye. His lean fingers seemed burned by the sun; they were rough and black next to the soft white flowers. The smell of jasmine filled the place and they drew it deeply into their lungs. Miriam sighed. She handed him a five-pound note. His white teeth lit up in a smile. He handed her three jasmine necklaces.

She tenderly returned them. "Keep them for yourself."

The smile faded from his dark face and his lips were parted by a soft voice with broken words.

"I ... am not ... a beggar."

He placed the three jasmine necklaces back on the table and ran away, calling *jasmine, jasmine*, with a voice like a bird's.

Groups of young men and women walked alongside the Nile. The men had shaved heads and the women covered their hair with white or colored scarves. Their eyes were lined with kohl, their lips colored red, and their legs squeezed into tight jeans. They swayed on high heels. They held the hands of the young men and exchanged kisses and embraces under moonlight that slipped between transparent clouds. Miriam the poet hummed words of her own making.

Love breaks the laws of heaven and earth
and the veil falls from the face of the moon.

Gamalat shuddered with her eyes half open. She woke from her drunkenness for a brief moment and murmured, "May the almighty God forgive our mighty sins."

⁂

Roustum used to invite the young woman to dinner at a small restaurant by the pyramids. She arrived late, following Gamalat's advice: "A man's desire is kindled by waiting for a woman. Waiting kindles love like fuel feeds fire."

She spotted him sitting with a book, his eyes wandering past the pyramids and the Sphinx. He'd left Carmen at home working on her novel. He used to tell her about his other relationships, for honesty's sake, when he got home after midnight and climbed in bed and embraced her. He showered her with kisses, hoping for forgiveness, and performed his prayers, his ritual of asking for faith and help.

He rose as he saw the young woman approaching. He kissed her on the cheek. She felt his warm lips on her face. Her fingertips were cold despite the hot weather.

Carmen used to tell her that she was cold-blooded and warm-hearted, just like the English.

Carmen did not know that she suffered from anemia because of a lack of vitamin B in her diet, and an iron deficiency, along with a growing sadness.

Roustum pulled out a chair for her. He did not sit back down until she was comfortably seated. She was not used to such tender treatment from Samih. Maybe he had behaved like this in the early days of their love, before their relationship had dwindled into the ordinary. Life had become tepid, like water from a tap. That shiver in the body and the rapid beating of the heart were over. Samih had forgotten his promise of marriage during their engagement and she made herself forget it in the name of independence and freedom.

علىٰ

The young woman started writing her novel the same week she arrived in Barcelona. The baby moved inside her. A small foot kicked against the wall of her womb from inside, one kick after another, one word after another in the mysterious novel she was trying to write. She recalled Samih's features. He was packing his suitcase to leave forever. Carmen lay in a mental hospital tied with ropes to the bedrails. When she saw the young woman entering the room, her face lit up with a smile. She had lost weight and the sparkle in her eyes. The joyful ring in her voice was gone and she complained of the doctors' ignorance.

"They think that my husband is the problem in my life and I tell them that it is not Roustum, nor any other man. The problem is greater than all men combined. The problem has to do with me, Carmen the writer, not Carmen the woman."

The young woman avoided looking into her eyes. Carmen's eyes seemed tired and filled with an old, hidden sorrow. Talking used up her energy.

Carmen reached out her frail hand and held the young woman's. "Roustum cannot come between us. Friendship between women is stronger than the love between the sexes."

"Roustum loves you, Carmen. You are his only love."

"There is nothing called the one true love. Life by nature is varied. This idea of an exclusive oneness is a disease inherited from slavery."

She pointed at the closet with a pale finger. "Open it and take the pages of my novel. They took it from me by force and locked it up. They say it is inspired by the devil, that all arts are inspired by the devil, even poetry. The doctors in this hospital are like policemen. If it were not for Roustum, they would have put me in prison."

"Carmen, you have to be sure of Roustum's love."

"Love does not preoccupy me, I have more important concerns."

"Roustum never lied to you, Carmen."

"Love does not know of truth or lying. Love is above morality." She smiled in fatigue. Her blue eyes wandered away. The desert of Helwan was visible from the window, stretching to the horizon like a sea of yellow sand. It shone under the sun like the water of the Mediterranean.

She kept holding the young woman's hand. Her long and elegant fingers were a little shaky. There was a table beside her bed with medicine bottles bearing many Latin names. Her eyes stopped at the word *Seroxat*. She had noticed this name on one of the bottles in Gamalat's room. She'd taken one pill every night to fight insomnia and nightmares and the fear of hellfire after death.

~❧~

It was summer when Samih left. The young woman imagined that Roustum would go back to Carmen. The word *loss* had always frightened her. She could bear losing Roustum, but not Samih. Friendship was more reassuring than love, a calm ship on a raging sea.

27

"Carmen loves Roustum without a doubt, though she believes in socialism and sharing," Samih had said. He laughed sarcastically. "Oneness is the fantasy of an unsound mind, itself a duality of love and freedom, disease and madness. In our imagination, all is transformed into grief and sorrow by forgetfulness."

During the lonely nights in her small room the young woman did not know where she was. She only heard the beating of her pulse and ticking of the clock near her head. She was losing speech, in Arabic and in Catalan. Words evaded her. She was unable to write down a single letter on paper. The novel deserted her just as she had deserted it. Many things carried her mind away from writing. Demonstrators were shouting in the streets of Barcelona, in Catalonia Square. Their voices came through her closed window: *Guerra no, Guerra no, Iraq. Guerra no, Palestine*, George Bush *assassí*, Tony Blair *assassí*, Aznar, *assassí*."

Assassí means killer in Catalan. Blood rushed through her veins. She felt it rising hot to her head. She went into the street, quickly heading from Antonio Lopez Square to Columbus Square. Tall trees lined both sides of the road. The buildings were the old Catalonian style. Huge pillars were topped with statues. High round towers scraped the sky with their points. The statue of Columbus stood proudly in the distance, surrounded by statues that looked like angels and women with wings. The ground was teeming with bodies, endless crowds of men and women marching from the Ramblas to Catalonia Square. They marched in all the streets, gathering in all the squares, thousands, millions, carrying banners written in Catalan: *Guerra no, Guerra no*. Their voices shook heaven and earth: *Assassí, assassí* . . .

Her body melted into the crowd and her voice rose with the rest: *Assassí, assassí*. Tears welled up in her eyes. She stealthily wiped them away. She'd been ashamed of her tears since childhood, as if they were a fault. Tears flowing freely in joy, then drying, trapped in sorrow. Joy melting into sorrow and tears flowing into the serenity of a river. She thought of Carmen tied with rope to the bedrails, her eyes wandering in the sands of the desert, the bottle of Seroxat.

"Are these sleeping pills, Carmen?"

"They call them antidepressants. Three nurses force my mouth open. I hide them under my tongue or in my mouth. A life of depression is better than life in a hospital. They call me crazy."

"Your mind is worth all of theirs combined."

"I think of committing suicide."

"That is madness."

"No, it is the epitome of sanity."

Carmen's voice reached her at night across the sea. The waves in Barcelona gently touched the shore and left again like the fingertips of a sleepy mother. She reached out to touch her child. She made sure she was there. She was afraid to lose her in her sleep. Her hand reached out and touched the child inside her. She made sure she was real, felt by hand, neither dream nor hallucination. Before she was aware of her, her belly had swollen with pregnancy. They took her to an underground clinic. They bound her with rope and injected her with an anesthetic. She opened her eyes after an unknown length of time. She saw a piece of her flesh in a bucket of blood.

That deep wound in her guts, she could almost feel it. Roustum used to kiss it with his lips before he kissed her. Carmen used to take contraceptive pills.

"The world is filled with millions of children who die of hunger and war. Roustum wants a child to carry his father's and his grandfather's name."

Roustum would whisper in her ear as he embraced her. "I want a child who looks like you, Carmen."

༺ཞ

The young woman looked out at the sea and the mountain from the rooftop. The statue of Columbus, the small boats near the shore. The heads of statues in the streets and the squares. Not a single street is without a statue of a man or a woman from history: writers, poets, artists. Galleries displaying their work are everywhere. Paintings by

Salvador Dali, for his centenary. Ads for a film by Pedro Almodóvar, *La Mala Educación*.

Annajell was ringing the doorbell. She was a student at Barcelona University who came every Sunday to mop the roof and the stairs. Yolanda paid her in plates of paella instead of euros. She volunteered to mop the young woman's floor for free. The young woman would make her a cup of green tea and serve her a slice of cake. They would sit on the wooden bench on the rooftop. The sun flooded them as they drank the hot tea. Annajell told her story using sign language and a mixture of Arabic and Catalan. Her name was Annajell Carlos Isabelle. She carried her father's name, Carlos, and her mother's name, Isabelle, according to Catalonian custom.

"But I am more proud of my mother's name than my father's. My mother is the one who brought me up after my father left. Do you carry your mother's name?"

"Our law does not recognize the mother's name."

"That is a catastrophe."

Annajell's eyes moved over the young woman's obscured belly, hidden under the wide shirt. "Did you come to Barcelona for her sake?"

The young woman pointed at the pages of her novel that were stacked on the floor in her room. "I have also come for its sake."

Though writing seemed to her to be pointless. Words on paper were like words in the wind, she thought: they didn't become real, didn't become action, as words of love do.

The first person who had really drawn her attention to writing was Miriam the poet.

"Our wounds can never heal except through writing," Miriam said. "Nothing can overcome madness or death except writing.

She recalled Miriam's voice speaking those words. Her black eyes sparkled with light in the darkness of the night. There was neither moon nor stars, as if the light came from a place at the back of her head. Carmen appeared to her, too, but with less force. She remembered her as she had been before she went to the hospital. She wanted her to be her old self, with light in her eyes. She also wanted to recollect Samih's pale dark face, his clear green eyes, like the plants of spring.

༄

Before she met Roustum she'd led a quiet life. Samih gave her the love she needed and more. They had a soft but strong relationship, like an eternal thread of silk. She was bored with eternal things. Samih was unable to break the cocoon around her soul. He never elicited the mysterious spring in her depths. She was overcome with boredom when she was with him. Yet she longed for him in his absence. She used to disappear for a while in order to understand herself, and then return. She took refuge in him from despair and the desire to die. She accused herself of being ungrateful, and asked for his forgiveness. He used to take her in his arms like a mother. He never blamed or rebuked her. He would tell her that she was a free person, that she could come and go as she pleased. But freedom seemed to her a disease she wanted to be rid of. She walked hungry in the streets without a job, without hope, and without a safe place to sleep, protected from the eyes of men. Days passed without food, with only the dust in the streets and alleys filling her mouth and nose.

Samih entered her life like a breeze that enters the lungs of someone deprived of air. She threw herself into his arms out of necessity, out of a desire for life and safety and a longing for love. She was like the desert, which longs for the drops of rain it receives as a gift from heaven, but cannot return the gift because it has no water, not because the generosity of its nature had failed.

She got used to seeing Samih. His green eyes became part of her life. He would drive her in his gray Renault to her job at the orphanage. It was in a cul-de-sac, in a building about to collapse. She preferred walking on foot to riding in a car. It took twenty minutes of brisk walking from her house in the cul-de-sac in al-Sayyida to reach her the orphanage in the cul-de-sac in Fam al-Khaleej.

The early morning air was refreshing. She worked from eight in the morning to four in the afternoon. She spent eight hours among skeletons with the faces of children and the eyes of old people. She used to sit with them in the dark room with black walls, or in the narrow courtyard in the dust, under the burning sun, where flies and fleas feasted on their blood. She used to wear a wide shirt and linen trousers and old leather walking shoes. She used to save the bus fare to buy a book or paper. In her mind was a mysterious novel. She did not know how to write it or how it began.

❦

Al-Sharq Bookshop was at the corner of Kasr al-Aini Street and Fam al-Khaleej. The owner was named Hafiz. He was short, thin, and hunchbacked. His eyes bulged behind thick glasses as he sipped his tea, puffed on a hookah, and read. He lifted his eyes from his book when she entered. She skimmed the bookshelves, reading the titles, and he dusted off books before handing them to her. She stuck her hand in her pocket in search of absent money. When she returned the book to him, he would give it back impatiently.

"Pay what you've got now and the rest next time."

If she had nothing at all he would smile wearily.

"You can borrow it, but under one condition: that you return it in one week."

The young woman met Samih for the first time in this bookshop. He used to go there to buy old books. Hafiz would invite him for a cup of tea and drag him into conversation about Arab philosophers, of whom the most important for him was Averroes, the father of modern medicine. Samih would grow impatient speaking with him. He looked at him as if he were contemplating a piece of antiquity in a museum. He drank the dark tea unwillingly, not showing his discomfort out of courtesy, or kindness, or sensitivity for the feelings of others.

One day she was flipping through an old book bearing the title *Muqadimat Ibn Khaldoun* when she heard a voice behind her.

"May I give you the book?"

She knew nothing about Ibn Khaldoun and she knew nothing about Samih.

She had seen him more than once at the bookshop without paying much attention to him. He had subdued features that did not summon surprise. They did not force one to awake suddenly from the sea of daily routine. Day after day passed without anything out of the ordinary making her stop and take notice. Not a face that excited her imagination or a book that stirred her mind. Time passed quietly, stagnant, like the Nile on hot days, with not a single breeze to move the leaves on the trees. There was no air and the trees were cut down. Houses were held together by concrete. There was no green. The streets were made of black tar. Miriam the poet called Cairo a city of concrete in her poem "My Cairo."

The young woman read Ibn Khaldoun from the first page to the last. She understood very little of the book. It was the first thing that brought her and Samih together inside al-Sharq Bookshop where the air was stale and filled with dust, smoke from the hookah, and the smell of hashish.

Samih seemed different to her. His clothes and appearance were tidy. She did not look in the mirror. She was unsettled and lived in anxiety. He lived in comfort and quiet in a spacious apartment that overlooked the Nile in Garden City, next to the house where Carmen and Roustum lived. She lived in a dark room in an alley surrounded by loudspeakers that blared day and night.

Samih was attracted to her as anything is attracted to its opposite. She became attracted to him like a butterfly attracted to light, not like a woman attracted to a man.

⁓

The little girl stared at her with big eyes, as if she were staring at herself. She had seen those eyes when she was a child, in the mirror, or in the imagination. Her dress was the color of the earth and her thin arms were the color of burned wood. Her knees protruded and were covered with scratches and bruises. Her features had been carved in stone with a chisel. She was an orphan of the desert. Her black irises were like two stars shining in a dark sky.

The director of the orphanage sat behind a dingy wooden desk that took up half the space in the room. Her huge body was hidden under a black tent that covered her from head to toe. Her eyes were like two holes sunk into a mass of black, and like the eyes of a mouse or a fox in a trap they never stopped vibrating. She had a long wooden cane as thin as the switch she used to sting the children's thighs. She resembled a ghoul or the mighty black giant in myths and in *The Thousand and One Nights* and in the stories of jinn and blue ghosts.

In the burning hot days of the summer she used to sit in the courtyard under the shadow of a camphor tree. She would lift the black veil off her face to sip some black tea and wipe beads of sweat from her nose with the back of her black gloves. She would stick the end of the hookah in her mouth and smoke would pour from the two slits of her eyes. If Salvador Dali had seen her he would have painted her in the shape of a giant bat or a black hedgehog.

"Beware of the girl from whose eyes fire springs. She was born out of wedlock. Look at how she is standing and staring like someone who deserves to be shot in the eyes with a bullet!"

"She is just a poor girl, Miss Bogey."

"What? What did you say?"

"I am sorry, Miss Headmistress, it was a slip of the tongue!"

"You, whatsyourname, what do you mean by *a slip of the tongue?*"

"It was a mistake, dear Headmistress, only God is without error."

Her two buried eyes lit with anger. The children all called her Miss Bogey behind her back, and now she had done it to her face. *Only God is without error*: she used to repeat this phrase whenever she forgot something.

"Listen, whatsyourname," the headmistress always pretended to have forgotten her name because of her many distracting responsibilities. "I forbid you to utter this name 'Miss Bogey' ever again. Do you understand?"

Her lips remained sealed. She did not even nod her head, as she didn't want to give in to her power as the others did.

The headmistress's body kept shaking under her black tent.

"Understood?"

Her husband resembled her greatly. He was huge and wore a black cloak over his white jalabiya. He had a big head covered with black curly hair. His face was hidden under a black forest of long, thick beard that bristled like barbed wire down his chest. His eyes were small and sunken behind the black chaos.

He used to sit in her office and wait for her until she finished her important tasks. She deliberately made herself busy with the papers placed on top of her desk. She used to ring a bell and call for the cleaners and other staff, giving out orders with dos and don'ts. Her voice rose in blame and rebuke, as she watched her husband out of the corner of her eye. She loved to exercise power before his very eyes. He exerted power over her at home and she did not know how to avenge herself, except in this manner in her office, in this indirect way.

The little girl disappeared one day from the orphanage. Her eyes were carved into the young woman's memory. Her eyes had the luster of stars, and her features were stony. Her name was Sabah. She asked the headmistress about her. With eyes moving deep in the two holes, she waved her black-gloved hand.

"She has run away, let her go to hell!"

There were hundreds of children in the orphanage. The world spat them out just like it spat out stray dogs. No one visited them, no one healed them when they became ill, no one buried them when they died, and no one searched for them if they ran away or were sold in slave markets. The gangs who worked in that trade were part of the same underground (and above-ground) mafia that bought and sold weapons, drugs, and sex. The price of children changed with the fluctuations of currencies and stock markets. Barren women from the north journeyed south to buy children with dark eyes for the sake of motherhood.

The headmistress was paid in hard cash. She bought a ticket every year to go to Mecca for circumambulation around the Kaaba, to kiss the black stone, to repel Satan by casting pebbles, and to drink from the water of Zamzam and return pure with her sins forgiven, like a newborn baby.

"Your job at the orphanage does not suit you," Samih said as he held her in his arms. "You deserve better."

"A better job requires a high recommendation."

"I'll get it for you."

Roustum had invited them for dinner at the club in the Lido around the small swimming pool. She sat with him and Samih. Carmen was swimming. Her body looked slender in her red bathing suit with white flowers. She moved her arms and legs underwater like the fins of a golden fish.

The young woman tilted back her head and closed her eyes. She let the warm sun cover her eyelids. The air smelled of trees and chlorinated water. Men and women stretched out on reclining chairs as they made conversation. They were massaging their bodies with lotion and leisurely sipping lemon ice. Before them lay plates of barbecued chicken, béchamel pasta, fried lamb ribs, and a salad with shining cucumbers, green lettuce, and red tomatoes. The smell of barbecue rose with their laughter. It was as if she had traveled from one country to another, from the cul-de-sac in al-Sayyida to the club in the Lido. The waiter came carrying the menu. He was a slender young man. His white teeth shone in his brown face as he handed Roustum the menu written in a language she did not know, listing foods she had never heard of. She looked at Samih, who was engrossed in conversation with Roustum about *Wide Sargasso Sea*.

A feeling of estrangement spread through her body like a cold wind. She yearned for her room in the alley, with the smell of lentil soup rising in the kitchen and Gamalat's voice calling her, "I made some soup, you will lick your fingers after tasting it."

The waiter asked what she would like.

"Some lentil soup and green salad, please."

Samih asked for fried fish with tahini sauce. Roustum ordered some spaghetti for himself and Carmen, and escalope and another dish whose name she did not catch.

Carmen came out of the water and stretched under the sun, her body dripping. She smoothed lotion over her arms and legs. She moved as unselfconsciously in her bathing suit as if she were fully dressed. She devoured the food with the open appetite of a child, then threw herself back into the water. She went a long distance underwater before rising to the surface.

"Come have a dip, the water is lovely."

"She is trying to tease you, just ignore her," Samih whispered in her ear.

She felt more estranged than at the orphanage. She hung like a piece of straw in the middle of things. She did not like poverty or wealth. She wanted to be enveloped by a big warm heart, and a small peaceful house, to sleep soundly without being bitten by fleas, without being disturbed by loudspeakers. She wanted to see the trees and the sea from her window and make the dreams of her childhood (although she no longer knew what they were) come true. She'd had no childhood, no mother, father, sisters, brothers, or grandmother to tell her the story of al-Shater Hassan or play the game of the fox goes round and round with her.

Samih had said to her, "You speak about freedom without being free. You think of the future and live in the past. You and I have promised to be honest, to be free to choose. I don't compel you to accept anything—you are completely free. You are free."

The word *free* rang in her ears as disgraceful and the difference between them collapsed. A prisoner lived inside her who did not know freedom, who did not possess her body, who could not give herself until she had received a stamped document, a specified fee, a dowry, a wedding ring, and money enough to cover the cost of the electricity, the bed, and the rent.

Gamalat had said, "A man does not know the value of a woman if he has not paid expensively for her. The higher your price, the more you are worth."

Miriam the poet objected, "No! My worth is above that of property and money. I am not a product to be bought and sold in the market."

Gamalat laughed sarcastically and shook her veil-covered head. "And who are you, my dear?"

"I am Miriam the poet!"

Her voice, filled with dignity, rang strongly in the young woman's ears: *I am Miriam the poet*. Her eyes shone brightly in her rosy skin that was like the clay on the banks of the Nile, as she swung her hair confidently over her shoulders. Her head moved with pride.

I am Miriam the poet,
I sprang like a plant from the earth,
Without a family, mother or father,
Without a home, a lover or husband,
With only poetry!

As she sat in the Nile Casino she felt her body rising above her, taking her soul and mind with it, as if an unknown force had lifted her above the boat and the river, above the rooftops of houses and tall buildings, above the city of Cairo and the fields of the Delta. She closed her eyes as if she were sleeping and drifted in space without wings, flying above the clouds, above the Mediterranean, and landed on a new shore whose name she did not know. Everything around her was new, even her own face.

She looked at her face in the mirror. It was not the same old sorry face. She ran down the stairs and devoured the hot paella, then crossed Columbus Street and walked down the Ramblas amid the flowers and groups of young men. She went from street to street looking at buildings that seem like museums—Casa Batlló, Casa Milà.

Antonio Gaudí died years ago but is still alive in every work he left behind, even in the huge building they call the Sagrada Familia, which he never got to finish.

She spent hours in the big library in Catalonia Square reading the story of Don Quixote and the poetry of García Lorca. She contemplated the paintings of Picasso, Dali, and Miró and walked along the Port Olympic shore before returning home to shed all of her clothes except for the tiny bathing suit that hid nothing from the sun except her black pubic hair. Annajell took her to another beach where people did not wear bathing suits at all. The golden rays reached every part of her body. Men and women swam like fish in the sea. They stretched under the sun without cover. No one looked at anyone else. Everyone moved with ease, as if newly born. Their feet left similar footprints on the sand. There was no difference between male and female, rich and poor, atheist and believer, black and white.

A long sigh rose from deep inside as she lay on her back soaking in the sun. The heat penetrated her skin and opened every last pore. The same heat from thousands of years ago, from the first Pharaoh to the last one. His face chased her in her sleep. His picture in the newspaper left on the step. Gamalat picked it up with her fingertips, as if she were picking up a dead cockroach. She quickly glanced at the picture on the front page with half-closed eyes, opening her wide mouth to yawn, audibly cracking her bones.

"May God strike that tyrant dead!"

Then Gamalat threw the paper on the ground and stepped on it with her plastic slippers, as if she were finally crushing the cockroach. In fact, their flat was filled with cockroaches, like all the flats in al-Sayyida. Cockroaches once belonged to the family of crawling insects, then over time they started developing wings. They were black or a dark rusty iron yellow. They fed on fleas, ants, cheese, butter. They went down the gutter and swam in water without fins. Their mustaches were like antennas and recognized the smell of sour food, which they passed over without eating. The smell of musk in Gamalat's pillow used to attract them. Before she went to sleep she would take off her plastic slippers and hit them, one after another, screaming.

"May God do away with all the cockroaches, and the tyrant with them!"

God never answered her prayer. He sent her more cockroaches to multiply under her bed, and the tyrant remained on his throne. God was beside him with every step, blessing his glorious deeds. He would intervene if need be, to relieve his plight. He doubled his wealth and his votes in the free elections. Gamalat screamed as she hit the cockroach.

"The free, or the disgraceful?"

Miriam the poet was amazed when she heard Gamalat addressing the cockroaches and praying to God to strike the tyrant dead.

"Gamalat, God is with all tyrants, inside and out!"

"I ask the Almighty's forgiveness for every great sin."

Miriam the poet's laughter rose and rang in the young woman's ears, clearly and tenderly, like drops of rainwater. Her laughter sprang from deep inside her heart and soul. The young woman was unable to laugh like that. When she tried, her laughter was chopped and stifled. Her hand would rise to hide her mouth and keep it from laughing. She looked as if laughter had been piling up inside her from childhood, as if the minute she opened her mouth it would flow without ever stopping.

When Gamalat complained about the cock-roaches Miriam would say, "Just thank God they are not scorpions or snakes."

"Please, Miriam, may God protect me—'scorpions and snakes'—I shiver when I hear their names spoken, as if I had heard the name of Satan."

"Have you ever seen Satan?"

"Never, thank God."

"Have you ever seen a scorpion or a snake?"

"Never, thank God."

"That's why they scare you, Gamalat."

Miriam read from her poem "Fear."

We fear God because we do not see him,
we fear the Devil because we do not see him,
we fear death because we do not see it,
this is why God hides behind a cloud,
why the Devil hides,

why death hides,
and why the one on the throne in the high-
walled palace hides.
Fear tied to ignorance possesses us from
childhood,
and common sense escapes us,
and we no longer see daylight.

❧

Before the young woman went to sleep, Gamalat
would sit on the edge of her bed and advise her
like a mother: "Don't listen to Miriam the poet.
Poets are tempted by the devil. God has ordered
you to cover up all of your body except your face
and palms. The veil is the first thing you will be
called to account for. It is a sacred duty you must
perform just like prayer if you want to go to
heaven, my dear."

Gamalat never believed in the veil that
covered the face. Her veil was the modern type. It
had evolved over time and its color and shape
changed. She delighted in adorning and beauti-
fying herself: "God is beautiful and He loves
beauty, my dear. If you have been afflicted then
cover up. Ugliness is a blemish and it should be
covered like a woman's head."

Gamalat moved from life to the afterlife with
one word, one letter. One movement of her veiled
head and she rose to the highest heaven. A slight
movement of her artificial eyelashes and she
returned to earth. She used to wink with her kohl-

47

lined eyes and say, "One hour for your God and one for your heart. Work in life as if you will live forever, and work for the afterlife as if you will die tomorrow."

Gamalat worked for an Islamic governmental newspaper. Her office was in a tall building near the bridge. Her window overlooked Cairo, from the top of the pyramids to al-Mokatam Mountain and Mohammed Ali's Castle. Papers, newspapers, and magazines were piled on top of her desk. Pictures of the heads of state mixed with pictures of dancers and adulterous pregnant women. She had a weekly column called "God of the Universe." The phrase "The Great and Almighty Allah" hung on the wall in a golden frame. The holy Quran with a gilded cover lay in one of her drawers, along with a box of powder, kohl, lipstick, red henna, musk, perfume, cloves, mint, and mastic gum.

The telephone never stopped ringing and visitors never stopped coming and going. Reporters, writers, poets, the male and female stars of Cairo traded news and jokes. One of them told the latest joke. He whispered in her ear. She was silent at first, then her laugh rang out, showing two rows of white teeth between two delicate red lips.

"May God deal with your devil, Bahy."

Bahy al-Din Boram was listed in her telephone book under the letter B. He had a regular book review column in the paper, and he helped her write her own column. He was squarely built, pale, and neatly dressed. His pointed shoes were polished. His nose was long and pointed like his shoes.

Miriam the poet was the one who noticed this resemblance.

"You can discover a man's personality from the shape of his nose and shoes."

Gamalat disagreed. "Only a man's extremities reveal his personality."

"You mean his fingers, Gamalat?"

"I mean his toes. Anyway, there is an affinity between the two."

Carmen saw things differently, maybe because she lived in Garden City and walked by the Nile where the rich people walked their dogs and she exercised in the club where the upper classes went, each one of them pulling a dog by a chain.

"I have noticed a great resemblance between men and their dogs, Gamalat."

"Is this a joke, Carmen?"

"No, it's a scientific fact, because a man and his dog live in the same environment under the same roof, like a man and his wife, and after some time they come to resemble one another."

Miriam burst out laughing.

"Then Roustum resembles you, Carmen?" Gamalat asked.

"Roustum and I do not live under the same roof. I can only live by myself with my manuscripts and my writing. Roustum understands me because he writes and understands what writing means."

What does writing mean? The question turned around and around in the young woman's head as she tried to sleep. Most people live without writing. They are successful at work, have property, land, and money, without writing. They live and die and go to heaven or hell without writing, and in Paradise there are no pens and paper.

The question pounded her head like a hammer. The novel lay on the floor near her bed, a stack of paper covered by dust, like a lifeless corpse. When she glanced at it, a cold shiver, like a shiver of death, ran through her body.

She no longer had a desire to live. She was losing the strength to fight. Her mind, body, and soul were paralyzed. She was incapable of doing anything, even loving. She had stopped seeing Samih, Roustum, Carmen, and Miriam. She closed the door to her room in Gamalat's face. Life was worth nothing, she did not deserve to live, let alone to write.

The doorbell rang. The postman carried a registered letter written in black ink and stamped with the eagle's seal. It was signed by the headmistress of the orphanage. "Due to your absence, now more than fifteen days, we have decided to discontinue your services."

She held the piece of paper in her hand the same way Gamalat held a dead cockroach. She threw it in the toilet and sighed with relief. She took a shower with hot water and soap to wash away her governmental post and erase from memory the headmistress's black tent, the pale faces of the children with their stunned eyes. But she could not erase the two sparkling eyes of Sabah, the child who had suddenly disappeared. Those eyes looked at her in her sleep, in her dreams, in the mirror she'd had when she was a child, as if they were her very own.

༄

Gamalat used to walk to her office. She would go from the alley to al-Mobtadayan Street. Everyone in the neighborhood knew her: shop owners, doormen, salesclerks at cigarette and newspaper and magazine kiosks, at poultry and falafel and sugar cane juice shops, and wandering vendors and beggars. Gamalat had lived in the neighborhood before she became a well-known journalist. Unemployed youth used to get her to mediate with the authorities, to secure them a job or a government post, or even a work contract overseas. They went up to her as she walked with her white veil wrapped around her head, and her thick dress revealed nothing and did not swing around her either in summer or in winter. Her plump body shook underneath her dress as she held her yellow leather handbag, which matched the color of her high heels. With her white round face, her thin arched eyebrows, her big, kohl-lined eyes, and her red lips constantly smiling as she greeted them, "Salaam to you, and God's mercy and blessings," Gamalat must have seemed a spirit from heaven that had descended to earth to make their dreams come true. One day she would return to heaven, discarding her body, and becoming a spirit again. No one in the neighborhood knew anything about her other life. They only knew that her husband had died a martyr for Allah and his country, and that she was his pure widow who was faithful to him during his lifetime and after his death, and that she never married again.

The young woman got to know more about Gamalat's other life when she began sharing the flat with her. Gamalat made her look at her private diary. She trusted her and treated her like a daughter or a younger sister. She gave her advice in matters of love and seemed to be an inexhaustible source of sexual knowledge. She warned her to beware of the smallest hidden details of a man's character, and sketched a scientific rendering of the male and female organs. After becoming intoxicated on wine, she would speak graphically of her experiences. She would sing Omar Khayyam, Abu Nawas, and the *Book of Youth* for her.

She was the daughter of Sheikh Imam al-Gammali, the major Islamic propagandist. He'd become a media star after the first Camp David treaty. He owned buildings and properties, until the assassinations and the killings of foreign tourists. Then he was arrested for crimes of sexual perversion and political corruption. He died in prison from grief. His properties were divided up among his old and new wives and his sons. He never knew their exact number. Gamalat was his only daughter from his first marriage. She relinquished her rights out of fear of her brothers. Her mother died before she got her position in journalism. She did not have an advanced degree; she'd made her way with the only weapons she possessed: her exuberant femininity and the veil of virtue.

Her office became a place for entertainment and for passing time. She sipped cardamom coffee she made herself on the little gas burner she took from the lower drawer of her desk, together with the kettle, coffee jar, and pack of Cleopatra cigarettes. In the last few years, a hookah had appeared in the corner of the room near the library. Her room filled with smoke and the smell of coffee and powder. The cigarette stubs accumulated in the ashtray on her desk with her red lips imprinted around every one. The visitors never stopped coming and going: male and female friends, admirers and lovers, and some female lovers. If she were alone she would read the papers and magazines or turn on the radio or the small television on the shelf, or she would look from her high window at the bridge, or out onto al-Tahrir Square.

Bahy al-Din Boram, who helped her write her column (and even sometimes wrote it for her), jumped up every time the cell phone rang in his pocket. He would go quickly to the farthest corner of the room with his left hand raised to his left ear. He whispered into the device hidden in the palm of his hand with his right ear facing the desk where Gamalat sat. His right eye caught the bright look in her eyes and her laughter rang in the air amidst the swirls of smoke.

"Who are you speaking to, naughty Bahy?"

Gamalat had not inherited her father's corruption. She was disposed toward virtue when she could afford to be. But she suffered from apathy and a lack of inspiration and yearned after lust and pleasure. Her life revolved around one thing: men. She was like a woman who had fallen into the talons of an impossible love and was caught in the grip of a man who was enraged, jealous, crude, and possessive.

A man for her was not a body she desired for a night or a series of nights: he became her universe. Strong shoulders under a thick suit, a wide chest with thick black hairs showing at a shirt's unbuttoned collar, an erection beneath the trousers, a rough voice tickling her ears with imaginative and obscene words, fingers with large knuckles crawling over her body, black or blue or green or hazel-brown eyes filled with debauchery, virtue, anger, contentment, seduction, and intimidation.

Gamalat knew many types of men. She said that what attracted her to a man was his humanity, not his penis. She did not make distinctions between men based on class, profession, or family background, nor between Arabs and foreigners, except for their piety. She knew the editor-in-chief as well as his chauffeur. She knew a prince and a waiter in a modest restaurant. She inherited from her mother and grandmother a thorough knowledge of the erotic arts. She had learned from experts how to appoint a bed, prepare a bath, rub the body and massage the sensitive parts, which movements most arouse men and make them lose their minds, what to say and when, and how to make certain sounds with her mouth and nose and utter both slang and elegant words. Gamalat slept with men from the upper and lower classes, foreign experts, heads of institutions, husbands of women famous in the sciences or the arts and husbands of virtuous women who stay at home, unemployed university graduates, rebellious high-school students, workers, farmers, and soldiers of the working class.

She laughed when she compared the government minister's and the waiter's performance in bed. The minister who was petrified of the president wanted the lights turned off. He feared the light and was ashamed of his naked body, his organ shriveled by longstanding repression. He fretted over his wallet, which was packed with money. The waiter took off his clothes in the light and tossed his undershirt and underpants on the floor, where the first letter of a long name was reflected. One letter after the other appeared in light: M c D O N A L D' S.

The letters glowed as a word for a moment, and then darkness was restored.

"Men who vie for power are weak in bed, hesitant, and unsure of themselves. But poor men who are not interested in power are endowed with hot blood and strength and do their utmost to give women pleasure," said Gamalat.

Gamalat judged a man's virility by the shape of his fingers and his nose. The men in power have short fingers and flat noses that lack sharpness and length. Their penises are almost a replica of their noses: short and flat, medium or less in length and prominence. She used to say: "Virility in bed has nothing to do with power, because virility does not need extraneous power."

Gamalat was trained to perceive men's hidden intentions. She became very attentive as she listened to political speeches. She claimed that a man's voice revealed the shape of his body. The solemn and strong voice that emphasizes words is completely the opposite in bed. And as for the Don Juans, the ones who go from one woman to another, Gamalat contended, they are the most defeated in bed.

༈

The young woman spent years of her life in Gamalat's apartment. Gamalat taught her to pray five times a day.

"Prayer erases sins, like visiting the Prophet's

grave in Mecca," she said. "But prayer does not require a plane ticket or any expenditures. It is just a daily practice that, once established, cannot be uprooted."

The young woman acquired from her the habits of praying and smoking. Gamalat gave her cigarettes in return for various services. Thursday night was the night of entertainment, the night of pleasure, an hour for one's heart and an hour for one's God. Friday was the day for the Lord, for praying in the mosque, for repentance.

On Thursday nights the alley and al-Mobtadayan Street became quiet. Al-Sayyida became peaceful. The poor stayed at home to rest after working all week long. They drank black tea and smoked the hookah. Their women massaged their feet in warm water and salt and then their rough hands rose to massage their exhausted bodies. Blood rushed to the tired and languishing organs; only by God's power did they awaken and become erect.

Gamalat would sleep until midday and then spend the afternoon preparing her room for Thursday night. She called it the night of relief. She would put musk oil on after her bath and then sit on a thick cushion on the floor with the cell phone held to her left ear while her right listened alertly for the doorbell.

Samih always came when the young woman needed him. He entered her life like a breeze let into a dungeon. He provided relief after long suppression.

They were both passing through crises from which they wanted to be released. Both of them suffered from despair. They had both come to dead ends with nothing left for them but to throw themselves into one another's arms, like someone drowning whose fingers reach for the shore.

There was another woman he had loved, but she had left him for another man, only for that other man to leave *her* for another woman. So she wanted to return to Samih. He almost forgave her. He had forgiven her twice before, but this third time he decided not to forgive her and not to let her return. Her name was Susan, though she was called Suzy.

He said that she was crazy with the desire to prove herself. Her mind was not at ease like Carmen's. She was searching for a purpose for her life. She had ideas foreign to the world of women.

"What is the world of women, Samih?"

"I don't know."

The young woman's relationship with Roustum was entering a dangerous, contradictory stage. Each of them was working to destroy the other through love. They were living in the junction between love and madness.

Madness led Roustum to a storm of ideas and writing. Philosophy won out over art in his novels. He contemplated the universe and wondered. He repeated questions from the times of Aristotle and Plato. He tried to mend the gap between the body and the spirit, between good and evil. He often gazed into the distance, and asked her about the contradictions in love.

His voice rattled with the search for truth. It was hoarse, with a cracked masculinity coupled with a destructive worrying that led to fear and the desire to save himself in any way, and to save Carmen with him. He loved her more because she was a writer like him.

"You are a woman and I am a man. I fell in love with you to save my love for Carmen. I do not want to lose her and I do not want to destroy myself. You are not the type who is destroyed by love."

"What kind of love, Roustum?"

She was attracted to Roustum for his weakness, contradictions, blunders, and hesitations. He was unable to hide his reality as Samih could.

"Roustum, the love between us is something different. It is a part of something bigger."

"And what is this thing that is bigger than love?"

The young woman never understood why every time she and Roustum split up they would start to meet again. They would get lost in conversation and wander on foot or in his Mercedes through the streets of Cairo. They would sit in small cafés in shabby neighborhoods drinking black tea and smoking the hookah until dawn. They would hide from Carmen and Samih. Their consciences pricked them with every meeting and so they often decided not to see one another again.

But this only brought them closer. They held hands like children as they nibbled on pumpkin seeds and lupine on the banks of the Nile. They sat on the rocks or the wooden benches and rented a room on the sea coast. They embraced all night long, trying uselessly to wear out their emotions. But it was as if neither love nor sex nor anything else could satisfy them. They only wanted to discover the unknown. But the unknown remained clouded. They were saddened by the ends of their nights and knew the bitterness of reality and the necessity of separating. If they were engulfed by a consuming love, they knew also that it was small and insufficient.

～※～

In spite of the distance, she could still smell his lavender shaving soap, see the titles of philosophy books on his library shelves, recall the exact words of their night-long debates about the existence of God. He never closed his eyes when she kissed him, but opened them wider. His eyes were filled with a great doubt that resembled madness. He surrounded himself with his books and novels like a patient surrounding himself with bottles of medicine, or an alcoholic with his wine. She used to hear his breath at night and something in his head pulsing, the blood rushed audibly to his brain, as clearly as she could hear the ticking of the watch around his wrist. His neck cracked.

Though his eyelids were shut, light shone from beneath them as if he could see with his eyes closed. He looked into the heart of the anxiety in his depths. She was overtaken by sleep for an hour or a little more. She opened her eyes and found him awake, his eyes wide, gazing at her. Now he was studying how she looked in sleep, trying to discover something he could not see in the light.

"I can't live under the same roof with Roustum," Carmen had told her. "I do not want to sleep under his gaze, under his open eyes that watch over me like the eyes of God. Nothing kills love more than living under the same roof, sharing the same bed, becoming as close as a touch, him gazing at your face while you are asleep, invading your room while you are writing, eating three meals a day with you, penetrating your body twice in the same night, listening to him snoring, seeing his crooked, protruding bones as he sits on the toilet seat in front of you and you hear the sound of his intestines and the rattling of his liver and spleen, and the sound of his cough hurts you and makes you sleepless."

"I have lived a life of freedom and independence since childhood," Roustum said. "No one shared my bedroom. I cannot commit myself to the fetters of love or marriage. I do not allow anyone to question me about where I am going, with whom, what I am drinking or writing. Nothing kills love more than being together too much, the presence of another person under my bedcovers, the presence of a woman I hear breathing all night long. I am irritated by the sound of her breathing as it stops and starts."

❦

The young woman stretched herself out on the sand under the sun on the coast near Barcelona. She released a long exhalation filled with smoke and dust and deeply inhaled the fresh air. She had crossed the Mediterranean from the south to the north. The plane carried her in four hours to another world: buildings decorated by statues, the original paintings of artists, books visible through library windows, music and light, and seafood restaurants with tablecloths as white as snow ironed and stretched below sparkling-clean plates and napkins folded into the shapes of flowers and sterilized spoons, forks, and knives. Crystal glasses sparkled in the sunlight next to bottles of a Catalonian wine and a Petrea chardonnay. Annajell liked the first and Francisco the second. They chose a table beside the sea. Francisco was going through a period of depression. He wanted to do something with his life besides stand in the street like a statue. He'd once dreamed of becoming a famous artist like Salvador Dali, having gallery shows in different countries and becoming rich, with women hanging on him. A sick masculine dream, Annajell told him.

Annajell glowed with happiness. Her smooth shoulders were bare under the sun. She wore a delicate blouse that showed her firm belly, snug jeans, and a wide green belt. She stretched her arms wide.

"I've finally found myself in poetry. I was lost until I read Maria-Mercè Marçal. As a child, she came from the countryside to Barcelona. She was poor like me. She was able to conquer poverty and the world with her poems. I like this one:

> I received three gifts from life:
> I was born a woman,
> poor,
> and oppressed,
> and that made my rebellion threefold.

Maria-Mercè Marçal died in the prime of her life, as a flower does. Annajell had met her before she died. Her features were engraved in her mind; she had fallen in love with her. She discovered that her dead mother was not dead, but alive and walking around, reading her poetry amidst crowds, and at night she would wrap her in her arms and return her to her childhood, and to her own mother's womb.

Francisco gulped his drink and surged like an angry sea. He pronounced Catalan in sharp phonemes, like bullets. He could not tolerate Annajell when she spoke about her women lovers. He pursed his lips in disgust. "Those cold lesbian women are sexually impotent and circumcised!"

Annajell was not circumcised. Her body was complete.

"You are impotent like the men in the north. Impotency stems from fear. I love Maria-Mercè Marçal because she is a poet and not because she is a woman. She captures my imagination more than men, although she is dead. There is something bigger even than love, Francisco."

Annajell reminded the young woman of Miriam the poet on the bank of the Nile. Miriam had stirred her imagination the first time she met her. Her skin was the rosy color of clay and her voice, as she recited poetry, was soft, yet solid like marble. She was tall and strongly built like a tree, with roots firmly in the ground and branches high in the sky. Her thick hair was the color of the night and she had big eyes that shone. Their color changed with the movement of the moon. Her neck was long and strong and she effortlessly carried her head erect. Her body moved naturally, as if it were made of another substance, something other than bones and flesh. Maybe her spirit.

༻

The young woman felt desperate, unable to prove herself. She felt weak and frail. Her body lost its natural immunity to disease. Viruses attacked her summer and winter. She sweated in the cold nights and shivered in the heat. She was cut off from Roustum, Samih, and Carmen. Gamalat shared the flat with her as if she were sharing her body. She lived with her under the same roof. Disputes resulted from their excessive closeness. She saw Gamalat's aging face every morning, without eyebrows and eyelashes. She heard her voice in the bathroom invoking God. She sat on the toilet for a long time because she was always constipated. She heard the sound of withheld gases in her intestines, the accumulated fats of beans, falafel, and pig's feet, the clinking of chains around her wrist and rosary beads colliding between her fingers, the squeaking in her teeth as she reiterated God's perfections.

Gamalat was happy when she saw the young woman ill in bed. She became more powerful when the young woman was weaker. She would dress up, wear perfume, and burn incense in front of her as she lay in bed. Her cell phone was stuck to her ear as she pursued her lovers. She started her conversation with God's name, Salaam, and ended by praising the Prophet Mohammed. Her voice rang loudly even when the young woman had closed the door or stuffed her ears with cotton or buried her head under the pillow. She heard Gamalat's voice filled with pleasure, and blood boiled in her veins. Gamalat's love of life confirmed her own depression. Gamalat's joy increased her own sadness. Gamalat would open the door and sit on the edge of the bed, smelling of powder and musk. She wore a string of pearls around her head veil and held a cigarette between her red lips. The smoke entered the young woman's lungs and made her feel more ill. She slept on her side, her back turned to Gamalat. The wooden bed squeaked under her weight, like a sick animal.

Gamalat tried to make her feel better. She told her that she was wilting like a flower and nothing would replenish her except faith, because disease comes from the devil.

"Please Gamalat, enough!"

"Wear the veil and you will be fine. Do not listen to the words of Satan. I was just like you before God guided me. Faith is a protection against disease. God will punish you in this world and in the life after and there is no cure for you, my dear, except to wear the veil."

Gamalat went to her office. The young woman slipped into her room in search of sleeping pills. On the table near her bed were many types of medicine, labeled in foreign languages with an Arabic translation. Pills for expelling gases, for preventing conception, for depression, for constipation, for digestion, for happiness... Finally she found the sleeping pills. She took three with a glass of water and fell into a deep sleep.

༈

She woke to Annajell's voice.

"Today is Saint George's Day. No one stays at home on the day of love."

They sipped wine on the roof under the sun. They went downstairs. It was midday. Yolanda was sitting in the restaurant eating hot paella. The statue of Antonio Lopez stood erect in its coat. To its right was a huge palace with two high towers decorated at the top with statues, angels, and women with wings. Four round pillars rose high above the entrance. The stairs were made of white marble and Catalan letters were engraved on the stone: Correos y Telegrafos. She remembered that Samih was waiting for a reply to his message.

"I want to send a fax to Cairo, Annajell."

They went inside the huge building. She wrote the fax in black ink:

Dear Samih,

Thank you for your kind letter and for your efforts to find me a decent job. I have been unable to get any kind of work here. I have written nothing in the novel. I will return to Cairo after I give birth to my baby girl. I will give her my name and my mother's name. The law here does not distinguish between the father's name and the mother's. Most children bear their mothers' names, even the new head of government, "Zapatero." Zapatero is his mother's name, Samih. Will there ever come a day in our country when a man can bear his mother's name without feeling ashamed?

Annajell took her hand. They walked among the crowds down the Ramblas.

Saint George's Day is the day of love. The

ground is covered with flowers and books. A man buys a red rose and gives it to one woman from among all the other women. The woman chooses a book from among all the books and gives it to the man she has chosen from among all the men in the world. Annajell stood in front of the Plaza Catalonia Library. She bought the poetry collection by Maria-Mercè Marçal and gave it to the young woman, with a red rose. The young woman bought the poetry of al-Khansa in Arabic and gave it to Annajell, with a red rose. Annajell was able to read and write Arabic. She was working on a comparative study of the Arabic and the Catalan poetry of love and freedom. She knew the poems of al-Khansa by heart. She called her the free female Arab poet because she had never given in to a tribal chief or to a husband. The thing that Annajell liked the most in ancient Arab history was the women's courage, even that of the slaves.

"Do you know the story?"

"Which story, Annajell?"

"Two slave girls stood in front of the Emir. One was his old slave girl and the other was a new one whom he had recently bought. Jealousy rose up between the two slaves. The old slave said: 'God prefers me as He says that it is the old ones who are esteemed.' The new slave answered: 'No, He prefers me over the old, as He says the final one is better than the first.' The Emir laughed so hard he had to lie on his back. He ordered that the two slaves get equal treatment, as the Prophet had done."

68

Annajell's laughter rang in her ears and the young woman remembered Gamalat's laughter in her "God of the Universe" column:

Dear God,
I have listened to the government's announcement in the People's Council concerning the general plan for the state and the budget. This is a government that strives for the sake of God to carry out a reform in accord with the American style. There is nothing more within my power than to raise my two hands to heaven, praying that God Almighty will save us from the exorbitant cost of living, and may He take the life of those who profit from spoiled meat, poisonous insecticides, liquidated companies, the sweat of hardworking people, deceptive investments, emigrating youth, the disgracefully shrinking Egyptian pound relative to the notorious dollar, stolen antiquities hidden in dark rooms, loan sharks and smugglers of billions, the lines of women in front of the bakery, the bubbles of promises that evaporate in the air, O Almighty God who is most Merciful and who Hears and is Generous.

"And who is Gamalat?"
"She was my housemate."
Annajell looked at her questioningly. *Housemate* in Catalan means husband or wife, or live-in lover.

"No, a family for us has only one form, Annajell. A man and a woman living under one roof, joined by a marriage certificate. Gamalat is a friend I shared the flat with. She writes a weekly column in the paper, in which she expresses her anger. She believes in God and in the Prophet Mohammed, in accord with the Sunni school. She's angry because Shi'a Muslims allow women to inherit property the same as men, and because Muslims in China pray at midday and perform sixteen prostrations instead of the usual four, except on Fridays, when it is two. She is strict about the veil, and conformity in any religious matter. As for worldly affairs, she believes in diverse choices."

The Ramblas was quite crowded. Annajell got lost in the crowd. People's bodies pulled her away while the young woman watched a woman who stood like a statue, performing a pantomime. Her skin was colored with a tar black substance. Her clothes were a transparent white. She held a white umbrella above her head. Her eyelashes were thick, black, and unmoving. Children gathered around her, so she smiled and her teeth showed white, as bright as the sun. Her eyes were black, filled with blackness. She once more solidified into a statue. The children threw some money into the big white hat placed at her feet.

The young woman saw her among the children, wearing a colorful dress with a flower necklace around her neck. Her big eyes shone like two stars. Her facial features were prominent, as if they were carved in stone. She had the same sad look in her eyes even though she smiled. The young woman had seen her in her sleep since her childhood. She had stared back at her ever since she had looked at her own face in the mirror.

"Sabah?"

The child looked at her in surprise and hesitation. A woman with a huge body pulled her away by the arm. She wore a gray hat with a red feather and had black sunglasses over her eyes. From behind the darkness peered two dark eyes, as if she were looking through the holes of a black veil.

The young woman spent the night with eyes wide open, remembering the faces in the orphanage. Annajell came in the morning. She told her that the cheapest children came from Ethiopia, Egypt, and the Sudan, and the most expensive children came from Russia, China, and Israel. The average cost of a small boy or girl was more than thirty thousand dollars.

༄

A letter arrived from Samih asking her to return. He was waiting for her and her baby with great longing. "She is our baby, don't you remember? Choose whatever name you like. Zapatero carries his mother's name and he is better than the kings and presidents who carry their fathers' names."

She also received a letter from Carmen asking her to return home with the baby girl. "She is the

71

daughter of the three of us: you, me, and Roustum. You are the original mother, I am the secondary mother, and the original father is Roustum. If you like, add Samih as a parent. This young girl is lucky: she has two mothers and two fathers."

❧

She felt her longing for home under her ribs, in the strong steady beating of her heart, along with the other beating in her belly. Inside her, a small part transformed into a girl who resembled her. She saw her with the ultrasound. The Catalonian doctor smiled.

"Congratulations, Nouria."

He called her by her mother's name. Nouria.

"She will be a beautiful child. What will you call her?"

"She will have my mother's name."

"You can add your father's name if you wish."

"I had no father."

The doctor laughed. "You are lucky, like me. I knew no one else but my mother, just like Zapatero. I carry her name and I am proud."

❧

Yolanda stared for a long time into the black shining eyes of the girl and sighed.

"In the name of the Father, the Son, and the Holy Spirit, this child is my grandchild. Her eyes are exactly like his eyes were when he was a baby, my Francisco. He has emigrated to Australia, and I have no news of him."

Yolanda drew the cross over her chest. "Thank you, God, for compensating me for my son with this girl. Her eyes are exactly his eyes, as if I were seeing my dear son in front of me."

Yolanda took the child in her arms and cried. Her voice quivered with the Lord's Prayer. "Our Father who art in Heaven, hallowed be Thy name, Thy kingdom come, Thy will be done on earth as it is in heaven... for Thine is the kingdom and the power and the glory forever. Amen." Yolanda wept, and then smiled as she looked into the eyes of the little girl, as if she had found her own lost self, as if she had gotten back her emigrating sons and daughters from all the countries of the world. Her Father, the Messiah, had returned them all to her, all at once, with one look into that child's eyes. Her name is Nouria, the name of her absent daughter. "By the name of the old Catalonian gods, Nouria, you have the Kingdom and Glory forever, O God of the Universe."

Miriam the poet sent her a poem entitled "The Brave Nouria." who came into the world in spite of the world, against the will of all. Nouria who came like a ray of sunlight. Nuclear power cannot prevent the sun from rising, or the beating of the heart under the ribs, or that small part inside the womb, or a word of love in a poem.

As for Gamalat, she sent nothing except one of her columns from the paper: "The Loss of the Islamic World's Honor."

O God of the Universe,

Save the honor of the nation from being lost. Corruption has grown in our countries and the orphanages and streets are filled with waifs and illegitimate children. O God, save a man's honor from the frivolity of conspicuous women. You have created woman out of a curved rib as the Prophet, peace be upon him, has said. If we try to put it straight it breaks, so have mercy on us God of the Universe, and do not publicize the scandals, disgraces, and violations of honor at Abu Ghraib prison, or the occupation of the land of Palestine, or the President's betrayal of the People's Congress, or the budget deficit and the increase of our debt, or our not bringing Shari'a to bear on the law. God, lend victory to the men of the resistance in Iraq, and to its women, for the Muslim woman warrior saves the nation's honor. Praise to you, God, who imparts his secret to the weakest of his creatures, and places a nation's honor in the hands of a woman, who saves it if she dies a martyr for the country, and wastes it if she falls and is tempted by the devil.

As they sipped tea on the roof under the sun, Annajell said, "Don't ever go back, Nouria. If you go back, your daughter might be kidnapped or killed. She is an innocent child who has not done anything, and you too will be punished. I beg you not to return. You are at home here. Home is where love is, and where there is freedom."

Yolanda took the child in her arms.

"My only granddaughter. I have no one other than her in the world. Don't go back. If you do, she will remain here, in her home among her people. This is her right and no power can deny her that right."

At night that small part beat under her ribs, and the faces of Samih, Roustum, Carmen, and Miriam returned to her. Even Gamalat's face, with the veil wrapped around her head and her thin eyebrows drawn with the tip of the pencil, her ringing laugher and her voice saying, "Congratulations on the new job, my dear."

Samih had found her a job as the librarian in a sports club. The young woman bought a pair of strong sports shoes. She walked for forty minutes in the early morning from her home to work. She would go from the alley that was drowned in sewage to al-Mobtadayan Street. She got lost in the crowd, the dust rising from beneath the wheels of cars, buses, motorcycles, bicycles, and horse carts. She crossed Kasr al-Aini Street as if she were drawn into a whirling sea, only to reappear on the opposing shore. She shook off the dust and her dread as she went into the neighborhood of Garden City. It seemed as if she were entering another country in another world where people lived in quiet behind high fences shaded by trees and by the bougainvillea blossoms that were as red as a gazelle's blood, in new buildings or old palaces with marble or stone columns of European design. She passed the British Embassy, which resembled a castle from the Middle Ages, behind a high fence, and the American Embassy with an even higher fence, topped with live wire and electronic cameras, monitoring equipment, and radar. She moved from Garden City to the banks of the Nile and filled her lungs with air. She walked on the pavement. The huge Meridien Hotel obscured the sky. She saw American women tourists with colored hats and the tops of their breasts exposed, whose men wore shorts and tee-shirts, women of the Gulf moving under dresses that resembled black tents as their eyes shone from the holes, while their men wore suits or jalabiyas and long beards. Their toes showed from their open sandals and the beads of their yellow rosaries danced between their fingers according to their sect or group, right or left or one of the middle. Gamalat belonged to a middle sect, according to the Prophet's teaching that we are a middle nation. Roustum vacillated between the left and the right. Samih moved from the opposition party to the government's. Carmen remained neutral and said that art is for art's sake and not for politics'. As for

Miriam the poet, she recited her poem entitled "The Age of Defeat and Hypocrisy."

> They carry out transactions
> in London, New York, and Tel Aviv,
> they compose long articles
>   about development and self sufficiency.
>
> They compete to kiss the hand
> of the president and the first lady.
>
> And I am called Miriam
> after the name of the pure Virgin,
> the daughter of sinful Eve.
>
> I drink wine and live with the devil
> to write poetry.

In front of Kasr al-Nile Bridge the buoys floated on the water as if yawning in relaxation. Small boats decorated with colors and banners stood ready to take tourists on excursions. They were guarded by young men from Upper Egypt. Their bones stood out under their black flaky skin, and their wide yellow eyes were filled with sadness. On the right is Shepheard's. It stands in the place of the hotel that burned down half a century ago or more, the day Cairo burned at the end of the monarchy. It is dwarfed by the huge structure of the Inter-Continental, itself in place of the old Semiramis.

The young woman turned left on the mighty bridge guarded by the two beastly lions. Above the bridge, flags fluttered, along with a picture of the President, suspended over the Arch of Victory, where the wind hits it from north and south, from east and west. "But God Almighty," Gamalat said, "keeps it secure with free elections and the referendum in which the faithful and loyal people have said *yes* with a 98.8 percent majority. Our democracy must be improving, since that percentage has gone down from 99.9 percent."

At the white building of the Opera House at the end of the bridge, guards (who come from the lower classes) stand erect in front of its doors. Their clothes shine, but their eyes are dull. Only the elite goes to the opera, the intellectuals, the thinkers who participate in the elections in the names of factions and political parties of different persuasions. Men wear colorful cravats. Women wear evening dresses with headscarves shaped into turbans. Perhaps their hair is uncovered and their necks and cleavage bare. The word *Allah* or blue eyes hang from golden chains as protection against the envious eye.

She turned off the main street onto a path shaded by the trees, to the back door where she entered the club with the other workers. She had a card with her picture and her name, with spaces for marital status, political affiliation, employment designation, religion, her father's and husband's professions, number of children, thumbprint, and criminal record. She used to leave all the spaces empty, not even checking male or female. She wrote in nothing.

The guard stared for a while at her card and asked her, puzzled, "Are you new here?"

"Yes."

"What do you do?"

"I work in the library."

"With Major General Subhi Pasha?"

Four terrifying words, and the most terrifying of all was *Pasha*, an old title from the Ottoman Empire. This was the title used by ministers, prime ministers, the Mamluks, and army leaders. And *Major General* had signified a high position in the army from the time the government was under military rule. It was no less frightful than the term *Brigadier General* was in the age of the monarchy.

She made her way along the arboretum. The horse-riding club was to her left. A spoiled child with a bottle in his mouth was riding a small white pony led by an attendant who was old and thin, his body burned by the sun and becoming black, dry, and cracked, as he blinked worn eyelashes, most of which had fallen out.

She walked in the horse-racing track. To her right and left, a spacious golf course stretched out. She went from the track to the big courtyard to the club's main entrance. She walked to the building with the new restaurant and the air-conditioned lounge on the first floor. She climbed the wide marble stairs to the second floor, where the library was.

She would sit in the clean library, which overlooked the garden they called the tea garden.

Its name had not changed since the days of the British occupation at the end of the century before the last. Gamalat became a member of the club. She did some walking in her white veil and swam in the water with a black, water-resistant veil. She pronounced *tea garden* with the tip of her tongue. The word *lido* she uttered faintly, as if it were somehow unbecoming. She said that the word came from the Arabic *layda*, meaning a woman suffering from nymphomania.

"What is nymphomania?"

"It means *layda*."

"And what does *layda* mean?"

"In the masculine, it means *lido*."

Gamalat laughed until her eyes teared and she wiped them with the tip of her white veil. The young woman found out that Lido was the name of the small swimming pool designated for the elder members in the club. The workers in the club were not allowed to swim in either the big or the small pool. They were also not allowed to sit in the tea garden, or anywhere else, or even use the toilets, restaurants, or playgrounds that were specially designated for the members.

The library became the young woman's special place. She stayed there from eight in the morning until four in the afternoon, the same hours she used to spend at the orphanage in Fam al-Khaleej. But the library was clean and free of fleas and enclosed by bookshelves. The big window overlooked tall trees and the tea garden, beyond which one could see the croquet field. Gamalat pronounced croquet *karkouba*, which meant decrepit old lady. She used to say that *karkouba* was playing croquet, a game for the elderly who are unable to run, like the rich elderly of the Shura Council. They walk slowly with their obese bodies and their buttocks heavy from sitting for long hours on comfortable seats, discussing politics. Some of them belonged to the government party, some were leftists, and some belonged to the Islamic group. Gamalat became one of the croquet players. She bent her fat body over the small ball as she struck it lightly. The ball would jump a meter, or half a meter, and Gamalat would slowly follow it with her head held high wrapped in a neat turban and her big buttocks stuffed inside tight jeans.

Very few of the members went to the library. Major General Subhi Pasha was absent most of the morning. He was squarely built, bare-headed, and wore a yellow training suit with black stripes. He had a Havana cigar in his mouth. He said that he was the hero of the July revolution, not Nasser. He had the documents and evidence to prove it. He knew secrets of the prevailing order that would turn the hair of young men gray. They forbade him to speak to the mass media. He was a tennis and squash champion. The post of library president was unsuitable for a man of his position, but he accepted the job because it was in the old club. He came to the club every day to play sports and meet with friends.

She had nothing to do except read. At four o'clock sharp she picked up her small handbag and went to the first floor, stopping in the restaurant's kitchen to drink a glass of water given to her by a waiter named Mohammed. He was a tall, thin man with a tender look in his eyes. She walked under the wooden trellis where cars were parked like crocodiles sleeping in the shade. The curved backs of the cars shone. She crossed the expansive golf course. The word *golf* rang strangely in her ears. Gamalat changed the word into *galanf*, meaning unsophisticated. She used to make fun of the *galanf* playing golf, by which she meant her boss at the paper. His father had polished shoes in front of al-Sayyida Mosque. He made it through elementary school and then got involved in the newspaper business by running up to cars selling papers. He became friends with a boy who worked as a carrier at the train station. After the monarchy was overthrown, he rose in the government through his friendships. He became the editor in chief, and his friend went into the army and became the president.

One day the young woman glimpsed Roustum from behind, playing golf. He was standing ready to hit the ball. His legs were long and extended inside his black trousers. He hit the ball with a strong and graceful swing. The ball flew like a small egg in the air. He followed it with his eyes until it fell far away, near the riding club. He hurried to it with long strides, followed by the boy who was pushing the small cart that carried the tall, slender clubs. The boy's face was thin and long and burned by the sun. It resembled the faces in the orphanage.

The young woman walked briskly, hiding her face with her handbag. She was afraid that Roustum might see her before she went out the back exit. She walked briskly for ten minutes until she had covered the distance to Kasr al-Nile Bridge, where she let her muscles relax and watched the small waves coming one after another like golden fish under the sun. She stood in the middle of the bridge and filled her lungs with air and looked at the tall buildings on either side of the bridge. The tallest building was the Semiramis InterContinental, with flags fluttering around it. She walked to the end of the bridge, then turned right into al-Cornish Street, returning to the road she had come from. She went through the quiet neighborhood of Garden City to noisy Kasr al-Aini Street, then on to al-Mobtadayan Street and finally to al-Sayyida Zaynab's Alley, as if crossing from shore to shore.

One morning Roustum came into the library. He wore a gray training suit and Adidas tennis shoes. The young woman was deeply immersed in reading. She lifted her head from the book and found him standing in front of her with his face tanned by the sun and his eyes brimming with strength and health.

Her eyes widened in surprise. He asked her the reason she had left him. They'd decided

83

together in their last meeting. How could he have forgotten? Was it his many preoccupations, the elections, the Shura Council, the new novel he was writing, his problems at home with Carmen?

"Roustum, how could you have forgotten?"

"Forgotten what?"

"The decision was made freely by both of us."

"Does love submit to will, my love?"

"Maybe."

"A will outside of our own?"

"I don't know."

"Is there a will outside of our own?"

"Maybe."

"You mean a divine force?"

"I don't know."

Roustum did not believe in any god, but he believed that there was some sort of power beyond the human, which he called spiritual. The young woman asked him the meaning of spirit. His eyes wandered away and he let out a long sigh and whispered that only God could know. He almost resembled Gamalat, when her eyes wandered to heaven, saying the same thing: that the spirit is only known by God. But Samih was never in doubt. He believed absolutely that nothing superseded the human being. Carmen, like Samih, believed in the mind. As for Miriam the poet, she asked why the will of Satan always wins, and why does beautiful poetry always come out of the devil's inspiration? As for love, like poetry, it is above vice and virtue and submits only to its own law.

The words of Miriam the poet encouraged her to live and filled her with the courage to follow her desires. The young woman liked sitting by the bank of the Nile under the light of the moon listening to poetry and to words of love. She loved reading and swimming in the sea. According to the rules of the club she was not allowed to swim in the Lido or in the other pool, the Piscine. She was not allowed to sit on the chairs in the tea garden or to drink a cup of coffee any place where the members sat. She carried a sandwich in her bag. If she became hungry she ate it quickly in the library, with a glass of water from the kitchen or a cup of tea carried by Mohammed the waiter, with his dark skin the color of the Nile's clay and his white teeth that shone like the sun in his thin face and his dark eyes that were filled with tenderness. He had graduated from Cairo University's faculty of arts. He had a master's degree in contemporary Arabic literature and was unable to get a job except as a waiter in the club's restaurant. He was not given monthly wages but lived on the tips the members gave him. He pronounced the word *tips* with the tip of his tongue. Tips were only given to servants. He wanted to free himself from such poverty and degradation. He had ripped up his university degree and thrown it into a wastebasket.

Mohammed stole a couple of moments and rushed up the stairs to the second floor. He hesitantly entered through the door of the library, his face lit by a smile. He borrowed a book for a day or two and gave her a cup of hot tea. He exchanged a couple of words with her as he stood there, before any of the observers noticed him. He used to call them the Control.

❧

One day she took her eyes from her book and saw a woman poised alertly, watching her like a tigress. She had composed her features in her imagination from Samih's description, but she was looking at her for the first time. She was alone in the library. The woman stood silently, watching her with two piercing eyes, with legs wide in a tight pair of slacks that resembled tiger's skin. She had never in her life seen a tiger except in pictures. The woman stood looking her over from head to toe. Her eyes stopped at her old shoes that were coated with the dust of al-Sayyida Zaynab. Her white finger with its long, red, accusing nail pointed at her.

"An ignoble person like you took Samih from me?"

She was unable to look at the face blotched with white and red makeup and green eye shadow. The woman had black lines defining her eyes and the whites of her eyes were yellowish and bulged out with a hint of red. The ends of her long hair were red and her thin red lips revealed shiny pointed teeth. She was panting and her voice had the sharpness of a metallic ring.

"You are ignoble!"

"And who are you?"

"I am your mistress, Madam Suzy."

It was like a comic scene in the theater. She was sitting in a chair, a spectator who had nothing to do with the play.

She offered her a seat. Susan hesitated in astonishment, then sat emphatically with legs crossed. Her upper leg moved involuntarily before her, with her shiny red shoes with pointed toes.

The young woman's eyes were fixed on the movement of the leg. She did not raise her eyes to the face blotched with makeup.

"You... what's your name?"

She remembered the director of the children's orphanage. She had the same tone, the same manner and movement of the head, the features of the face hidden under a heavy layer of makeup instead of a veil. The two opposing images joined together in one vision. Susan stopped moving her leg when she saw her smile.

Since working at the library she had decided to detach herself from her old life. She had stopped seeing Samih, Roustum, and Carmen. She realized that they belonged to a different class, one she did not want to belong to. Maybe she had an inferiority complex, or a feeling of guilt. Or she had discovered a new world in the library, the world of reading and writing. She seemed to have found her lost self. It was a new pleasure that went beyond worldly pleasures. She walked on into a world of reading and writing, as if she had been born again by another mother, in another country. After having been lost in the ocean, she was anchored to a new shore.

"You have to sever your relationship with Samih!"

The name *Samih* rang in her ear, and she tensed. The word seemed strange in that metallic voice. She almost asked her who Samih was, but the memory came back to her in time. She saw her mother's face when she was a crawling baby, as if *mother* and *Samih* were one name for something from the remote past.

She was silent long enough to swallow suppressed tears. She closed her eyes as if she were falling asleep. She woke up to a defeated and weak voice.

"I wronged Samih. I found out his worth after I lost him. Please help me get him back."

Susan's voice was stifled. She turned her head toward the window and swallowed her tears. She stood up, stretching the muscles of her tight body and forcefully moved her raised head as if shaking off a moment of weakness. She went out the door, stamping the ground with her heels, without turning back.

The young woman often saw her playing golf. She used to cross the green quickly and go out the back way. If the young woman saw her she would move her head with a greeting and Susan would move her head quickly in an involuntary nod, then bend her lithe body to strike the ball. They exchanged smiles when they met face to face. One day they stopped for a while and were about to talk, but they did not have the courage. They had nothing to talk about except Samih and his name was one that each of them was trying to forget.

The young woman saw her once sitting under a tree on the edge of the golf course. She was resting on the green grass on one of the club's white towels with green edges. She was bent over with closed eyelids, as if she were sleepy. Her right breast showed under her white shirt and her left knee rose to support her elbow and her head was bent down, supported by her palm.

She seemed lonely and sad. The young woman wanted to pat her gently on the head, to throw her head upon her breast and cry, but as soon as Susan opened her eyes she left, heading out the back way without seeing her.

~✤~

The young woman wished that she would one day have the confidence in herself to stride over the ground the way that Roustum did when he entered the small restaurant on the hill by the pyramids. He made his way between the small tables with the white tablecloths and sat at the table near the high perimeter that overlooks the city. His eyes gazed out the windows and every now and then toward the entrance, wondering if she would arrive as she had promised.

She kept her promise in spite of the decision to break up with him. Keeping away from one another only led to more desire, to a surge of energy in the spirit, the body, the mind, or someplace else. It gathered at a certain spot in her chest and pressed on her heart like trapped blood, then rushed forth in a moment of surprise with all of its force, like the steam that moves a train.

She went late to meet him, as Gamalat always advised. "The beautiful one must be late. The later you are, the greater the man's longing. Let him wait all his life. In the depth of the male lies the instinct of the hunter. The easy prey does not excite him."

Or: "Don't be stupid like a grape in the garden of Eden that falls by itself from the tree into the mouth of a pious man, without him exerting any effort!"

Then: a ringing laugh, contagious as an infectious disease. The young woman, despite herself, was overcome with laughter. She unconsciously laughed with Gamalat until their eyes teared.

Roustum filled their cups with wine and they filled their lungs with the desert air. They had an overwhelming desire to talk. They exchanged ideas about the wars in Iraq and in Afghanistan, the massacres in Palestine, the tragedies of the immigrants, corruption and bribery in the state, the lies being published, the collapse of virtue and the rise in crimes in the name of honor, the upcoming election for the Shura Council.

They talked to one another as friends talk. They started with political events and war and ended with art and literature. He was writing a long novel and he did not know how it would end. She was writing her first novel and she did not know how it would begin. She remembered little of these conversations but the light of the moon turning the faraway sand dunes into waves. And the smell of the desert and the wine and the lavender aftershave, before he kissed her. These moments had stayed with her despite the passage of years. They took over her imagination more than the crazy lust in bed. Those moments disappeared, despite their charge and force. Only the delicate touches remained in her memory, the faint smell of wine and lavender disappearing into the air, as if those were the truest moments.

On the other side of the wide sea, the young woman tried to capture these moments with the tip of her pen. Uselessly. The letters add luster to the page, then fade like stars fading in the light of the sun. They will be born again in the womb of night before fading again.

She used to sleep in Samih's arms in her room on al-Mobtadayan Street. The old wooden bed creaked under their bodies as they embraced. Gamalat's snoring reached them through the closed door. Her snoring was faint and regular, like the ticking of the clock near the bed. They woke up before dawn prayer to the sound of water in the bathroom and her voice as she intoned God's attributes. Her plastic slippers scuffled on the floor. She pulled the prayer rug from under the bed and spread it out on the floor in the direction of the Kaaba in Mecca. Only then a voice rose, calling the dawn prayer, followed by thousands of loudspeakers hanging in the old and the new mosques, firing like cannons.

Samih slept soundly. Nothing disturbed him. When she watched him with his eyes closed, he seemed peaceful. He smiled in his sleep. He circled in dreams like a happy child always assured by the presence of his mother and father, like an angel in heaven who knows nothing but goodness.

Roustum was different. His depths hid something evil. He held both noble deeds and large failings. He could be as cruel as a stone. Probably he resembled her more than Samih did.

She had cruelty in her, toward herself and toward others. She could say to Roustum without blinking: "Our relationship must end." She realized the danger of what heaved inside her. She wanted to freeze what was going on between them on the edge of friendship, keep exchanging ideas, what Roustum called "a mating of minds." Which he said was more dangerous than what happens in bed.

Carmen was his great love. The young woman loved her, too. Her imagination trembled at this thought when she was with him, sitting beside him in the restaurant by the pyramids. Her eyes searched in the desert and she asked herself what was the point of their relationship. She was a poor, worn-out worker with no credentials and he was an established professor, a man of the ruling elite. His wife was a distinguished writer from the upper class. The young woman sensed a scandal that could fill the city and destroy her life and his. The affair would end in separation, whether they chose it or not. The young woman expressed all this as they sat looking from the high stony edge into the bottomless pit. The houses of Cairo lay in the darkness below. The small scattered lights shivered like stars about to blink out.

He looked away from her. After a long silence, he said, "Is this a matter of our choosing?"

His voice rattled. She was addicted to his masculine hoarseness. It had a particular effect that moved something mysterious deep in her body and deep in her mind.

"Neither you nor I possess the power to choose—it is beyond our will."

"Not entirely beyond our will. It's part of the latent will in our subconscious."

Silence lingered between them and they heard a plane cross the sky, a car horn in the distance. He lit a cigarette with a match and let the match burn out. He contemplated the flame with his big eyes. The red flame was reflected in his blue eyes and the red melted in the blue like the sun sinking into the sea at sunset. Blackness crossed his eyes, and he became alert, as the flame burned out in his fingers. Darkness prevailed. The young woman could barely see him. She could only hear his hoarse whisper.

"I've promised Carmen a thousand times and every time I break my promise and return to you." He bent his head for a long while. The silence of the desert filled her ears with a long whistle, like sand winds blowing in from the east in the spring.

"And what does Samih think?"

Samih had told her, "These are matters in which promises are of no consequence, nor good intentions. I could never stand between you and Roustum the way Carmen does, not because she loves Roustum more than I love you, and not because I am saner than her, but because these matters are beyond the mind."

"Samih, you do not believe in anything that exceeds the mind. I mean the mind in the totality that includes the body and the soul and the unconscious."

"The unconscious?"

"I mean the collective forgotten unconscious."

The conversation continued between her and Samih in bed. They exchanged words with a desire greater than the desire to embrace. He said that she suffered from frigidity, despite her sensitivity and her hot mind. Her relationship with Roustum did not bother him. He saw that it was necessary.

"You are of a mettle stronger than the desire to possess, and your mind has room for more than one person. Maybe three or more."

Her mind rejoiced when she talked with him in the warm bed. She was overcome with a pleasure that surpassed sex and went beyond the spirit, beyond feelings of love, beyond masculinity and femininity. Yet this joy remained incomplete. It did not transcend the present moment: it barely moved from her head to her body. She felt something under her ribs, under her left lung, pricking like a needle under the artery that feeds the heart with blood, as if her body were infected by a mysterious chronic disease, and a voice from that spot whispered: "Samih does not love you. He is not pained that you have fallen in love with another man." She hit her breast with her fist. She wanted to destroy that voice, that hissing that reached her from a remote time, from the age of slaves.

Annajell held her hand as they walked in the streets of Barcelona that spring. The sun was bright. Thousands of voices shouted: "*Guerra no*, *Guerra no*, *assassí*, *assassí*, Iraq, Palestina." The streets were filled with women, men, teenagers, and children who held banners proclaiming, *Guerra no*, no to war, George Bush *assassí*, Tony Blair, Sharon and Aznar, *assassí*.

The demonstration had started in the big square at Fontanella on Lotana Street. They marched to the city center, joined there by other demonstrators coming from all the streets and public squares. Her body melted into the other bodies and her cracked voice became choked by tears. Arabic words mixed with Catalan, laughter mixed with tears. She cried for her missing self and her lost home. She was filled with sadness and joy at the same time. *Guerra no, Guerra no,* Iraq, Palestina. They were shouting on behalf of Iraq and Palestine. Although all these people were lived on another shore and were a different religion and color, nothing separated them. Millions of bodies, like waves of the sea rising and forming a single wave that juts into the sky. Helicopters circled, watching the demonstration with police eyes. Their metallic buzzing disappeared in the roaring of the human wave: *Guerra no, Guerra no, assassí, assassí!*

The sun was directly overhead, then it tilted toward sunset. Their throats dried up and their feet had swelled from walking.

"What do you think—shall we rest and eat a sandwich?" Annajell asked.

The café faced the parliament building. The young woman ordered a cup of tea with mint and an egg and cheese sandwich. Annajell ordered coffee with milk and a large sandwich.

"Have you been to see the parliament?" Annajell asked.

"No."

"Do you have a parliament?"

"Yes, but—"

The young woman did not continue her sentence. She wanted to say: "Our parliament is different from your parliament. We cannot decide elections. You were able to bring down Aznar in your last election."

"Zapatero was successful and he decided to pull our troops out of Iraq. Aznar was a murderer like George Bush and Tony Blair."

"Zapatero is his mother's name."

"You have real elections and a real parliament but—"

The young woman closed her lips. She recalled the building on Umma Council Street, and behind it the other building that housed the Shura Council. She saw Roustum coming out of the building and walking slowly, his eyes wandering, soft, yellow prayer beads in his hands. They resembled the rosary in Gamalat's hands. Gamalat had joined the Shura Council, just as she had joined the sports club. She became a member.

❧

The young woman stood in front of the parliament for a while without going in. The building was white and had Catalonian columns. In front of it was a small lake. Flowers and green leaves floated on the surface like dead fish. In the middle of the lake, a statue of a sitting woman, bent over in a broken pose, shone in the falling rain. She held her head in her hands and bent over her naked breasts. Her right knee was on the ground and her left knee hid her pubic hair. Her left breast was hidden but her right breast shyly showed under her arm. The name of the statue was engraved on the stone pedestal in Catalan:

Desconsol, sadness. The artist Josep Llimona had sculpted it in 1903, an entire century ago.

The young woman stood in front of the bending woman. She remembered Susan sitting under the tree in the club bent over herself in this sad posture. She realized that Susan's love for Samih was bigger than her own love for him. She missed him more. She deserved him more. She remembered Samih after he had packed his suitcase. He remained standing at the door. She did not lift her face to him. She let him go without an embrace, without a final word of farewell. She feared looking at him. If their eyes met, he might have pulled shut the door and come back in. Big love remains engraved on the heart's membrane, like a deep wound in the body.

In the mental hospital Carmen was angry with the doctors.

"These stupid people, they force me to take pills for happiness while keeping me from the source of my happiness. My only happiness comes from writing. People drink wine in search of happiness and I drink it to become sad. I have lacked nothing since Roustum returned to me. But the wounds of the heart do not heal like the wounds of the body. They are embedded in the brain, in the recesses of the mind. They are the wounds of the spirit."

The word *spirit* rings in the young woman's head, like a stone thrown in the water making endless circles, big circles with smaller circles inside. The small circles have smaller circles inside and the bigger circles have bigger circles around them. It is endless. The circles go around a deep spot in the middle, a whirlpool in the sea. The question pulses in her mind and circles with the intoxicating effect of red wine.

"And what is the spirit, Carmen?"

Eternity's chronic question.

Samih had mixed blood in his veins. His father was a believer in God and the Prophet. His mother believed in the Father, the Son, and the Holy Spirit. A Muslim man can marry any woman under one condition: that she belong to one of the main religions.

Samih walked with firm and quiet steps. He knew exactly where to place each foot. His features were sane and balanced. He believed in science and evidence, in experiment and hypothesis, in right and wrong. His eyes were green like the color of the plants in the fields in the Nile delta that are quiet and move softly with the breeze and shine with light when the sun shines.

Gamalat used to say that he had scientific features that were cerebral and devoid of emotion. She called him Professor. She told the young woman that his attraction to her came from his mind alone. She looked her over from head to toe and pursed her red lips and narrowed her kohl-lined eyes as she searched for something she would call femininity. She clapped her hands. "God has his own ways with his creations."

Her standards of beauty did not favor the young woman. She was too thin, a bag of bones, and dark blue like the Copts, whom she called infidels and blue bones. Her voice was hoarse and masculine. She did not have prominent breasts or a bottom like her own round one that shuddered with femininity every step she took.

The first time Samih visited, Gamalat glimpsed him through her slightly open door.

"Are you a Muslim or a Copt?"

"Neither this nor that."

"Good grief! A Jew?"

"No."

"Buddhist or Hindu?"

"Neither this nor that."

"What a catastrophe, what doom!"

Gamalat never entertained the thought that a human being could live without a religious identity, especially in Cairo, once the city of a thousand minarets and now maybe a million or more.

In thirty years, the city and the people had changed. In the sixties, Gamalat had not worn the veil. She used to have her hair styled at a salon. She repeated communist phrases about the differences between the classes being melted away. She repeated jargon. Then she converted overnight, with all the rest, during the age of the believer President. She became one of the propagators of an open Islamic policy. During the pilgrimage season, she used to travel to visit the grave of the Prophet and the duty-free shop. She returned loaded down with veils, rosaries, incense burners, see-through lace underwear, and prohibited videos. In the election season she gave them out to voters along with the Ramadan calendar. After the assassination, she denounced the old despot. She slipped like soft soap into the new party that bore the names nationalistic, patriotic, Arabic, Islamic, and moderate. Its members believed in realism and partnership, especially any partnership with God. It was a governmental party and a semi-governmental party at the same time. It was the legal opposition. They said *yes* in the elections and in the mass media they said *no*. They opposed everyone, except God and the President. God poured his favors onto them. Any money was God's money, and God gives to whomever He pleases, without any accounting.

Gamalat was not among those close to God, despite her daily prayer and her thick veil. She received no worldly favors, except for her weekly column and her monthly wages from the council, with a nominal compensation from the permanent committee.

She pursed her red lips and mumbled, "Nothing is permanent except God Almighty."

∾❧∾

Samih owned a publishing house in Heliopolis. He had inherited it along with a house in Garden City. The responsibilities of printing, publishing, and distributing took him away from his life's dream, which was to be a novelist, like Tolstoy or Dostoevsky. His dream kept him awake at night, but in the morning work burdened him. This inheritance from his father and his grandfather yoked him to the past. He threw himself into the business. But he hated calculations, numbers, assessments of gain and loss. He lost more than he made, and his face became thinner and paler, as if his heart bled as he sat at his desk.

He used to visit the young woman in her room in al-Sayyida. He seemed a stranger to the place with his clean, shiny shoes and his ironed suit. He preferred light blue colors or a calm gray. She sometimes visited him at Dar al-Nashr. At his big desk, his thin body and pale face looked to her like a prisoner inside the walls. He was buried in papers. Around him rose bookshelves from the floor to the ceiling. He lifted his head and saw her. He rose, smiling. His frame was strong and his back straight. He shook hands with a kindness that showed will power. He had a direct look, and a warm friendship brought him together with his workers, as if they were colleagues.

In the big hall, seminars about books and novels were held. Many people took part in them, a lot of men and women. Roustum was one, and

Carmen. She used to see them sitting among the audience, his head next to hers. They came and left together, his arm around her waist. One day he came alone. The seminar was about *The House of Spirits*, by Isabel Allende. A well-known critic moderated the conversation. He said it was a feminist novel that did not delve into significant human problems, but instead got lost in small feminine details.

Samih had given her the novel. The young woman lived for days and nights with it. Gamalat and Miriam the poet read it. The three friends gathered on the boat on the bank of the Nile to talk about the novel. Miriam said it was a beautiful novel; she had not read one like it in years. Gamalat called it a failure. She said it went against religion and morality. As for the young woman, she read the novel more than once, and stopped at certain parts to reread them and reconsider the meaning behind the words, beneath the lines, between the lines. Then she read about the life of the author Isabel Allende, whose father was once president of Chile.

The important critic was sitting on the platform. He was short and fat and his skin was white. His red bald head shone under the light. His tie was brightly colored, and she could see his tongue move when he said, "A feminist novel."

The young woman raised her hand to say something. She contradicted the important critic. Opposition was not familiar, except among the

103

elderly elite. He gave her a piercing look from behind his thick glasses. Her appearance did not indicate that she belonged to the elite. She was an unknown young woman, with a pale face. He waved his hand, as if he were shooing away a fly.

She was overcome with nervous sweat and humiliation, as if he had slapped her face. She began to run, as if ghosts were chasing her. She stopped at the end of al-Horiya Street, and went into a small café that sold sandwiches. She sat to catch her breath. She could see the street through the window and the glow of the sun setting behind the buildings. The houses in Heliopolis have stone pillars that resemble those of old villas. They have large balconies with wide windows draped with curtains and behind them she could see happy families: fathers, mothers, and children, laughing, girls and boys with plates of food on the table before them, the steam rising with their laughter.

The young woman looked around sadly. She cringed in pain. She had no family. She had no childhood. She had not eaten all day. The waiter came with a smile on his face like that of a kind mother. He asked her what she would like, and her answer came out choked with tears.

"A white cheese sandwich with olives and a cup of tea, please."

As she sipped the tea she saw a Mercedes come to a stop outside. Roustum stepped out, leaving the door open behind him. He headed toward the café with long, fast strides. He stood before her, placing his elbow on the table.

"I liked very much what you said. The novel is amazing and that critic is known to be ignorant of literature, especially feminist literature."

His voice was a little hoarse and had a rattle. She had a green olive between her teeth. It fell from her mouth before she could answer. The olive rolled on the table until it touched his hand. He took it between two fingers and threw it in his mouth, laughing.

"I love green olives very much. I left the car running. Bring your sandwich and olives and come with me. I want to introduce you to my wife, Carmen. Samih will join us after work."

༺༻

The young woman sat in the front beside him. The Mercedes took off smoothly, like a white ship gliding over water. Soft music was playing. Her tired body relaxed in the comfortable seat. The window on her right was double-paned and solid. It kept the noise away. Cairo appeared outside like a sea, with beating waves, with crowds of people, cars, bicycles, motorcycles. The city surged with movement. She could see it without hearing it, as though she was watching an old silent movie. She could see his profile to her left. He had a wide forehead tanned by the sun. He had a strong confident nose. His lips were closed in absorption and his eyes were fixed on the road at the same time as they seemed to wander elsewhere. Stubble showed on his face. He had not shaved for days.

From time to time, they exchanged a few words. He followed Latin American literature by men and women. He placed Isabel Allende alongside Gabriel García Márquez in stature. She would win a Nobel if there were any kind of justice.

Suddenly, she saw Gamalat walking in the street, before the car turned right into Kasr al-Aini Street and into Garden City. She was coming out of the grocery shop at the corner. Two black plastic bags hung from her hands and her head was wrapped in a white veil. She appeared before her as if she had sprung from the remote past.

The car stopped in front of a white villa overlooking the Nile. Branches of red bougainvillea hung from an iron fence and the smell of jasmine reached down the long passage to the front door. The inside hallway had carved stone pillars. A big chandelier with many small lamps like stars hung from the ceiling. Pictures in gilded frames filled the walls. A small hall led to a bigger hall then to another hall with a table. The candles on the table were lit. A servant as black as night in clothes as white as snow with a red velvet belt was laying out crystal cups, silver spoons, forks, and knives.

Carmen was in the library stretched out on the leather couch, reading. Rows of books in glass cases rose to the ceiling, surrounding her. She'd kicked off her shoes onto a soft decorative wool rug.

Carmen rose slowly and stretched. She was tall, neat, and seemed relaxed and fresh. The young woman shrank in her old dress, with her dusty shoes and her shabby bag, from which came the smell of pickled olives and the cheese sandwich. She felt ashamed. Carmen shook hands with her with an easy manner. Roustum opened a bottle of wine. The smell of barbecue came from the dining room. She was hit with a sad longing for the warmth of a family and a tranquil home.

Carmen sat at the head of the table. Roustum sat to her right and the young woman to her left. Carmen seemed to be the man of the house. Roustum was overshadowed by her, and absentminded.

The conversation revolved around the seminar, Isabel Allende's novel, and the important critic. Carmen laughed and said that he was ignorant about literature. She turned to the young woman. "Are you of the younger generation of writers?"

She shook her head. "I am not a writer, ma'am."

"Please don't call me *ma'am*."

"I am not a writer."

"A critic?"

"No."

"Then what?"

"Nothing."

Carmen looked her over with her big eyes, slowly, from head to toe. Her look almost resembled Gamalat's when she was searching for something attractive about her body. She found nothing of particular significance, so she shifted her eyes to her husband, as if seeing him for the first time. She looked at him keenly with her shining eyes. Her eyes stopped at the colorful tie that was knotted with extreme care. He only tied it like that on special occasions, such as during the election season, or in spring when flowers bloomed, and when something beat under his ribs.

Her eyes slipped down to his chest under the silk shirt and his belly that was pulled in by a leather belt with a silver buckle, to the four fastened buttons of his trousers. Her husband was an open book before her eyes. She read things in his eyes before they happened. She knew when he forgot to fasten the fourth button on his trousers. This happened whenever he wandered off into a new love story. Or during the election season, after having been in narrow bathrooms in the homes of voters.

Roustum sat relaxed, slowly sipping wine, his legs spread. Carmen had piercing eyes, and she fixed them on the tautness in his trousers. She looked at him with her inquisitive look, with her literary imagination, uncovering hidden secrets.

"You are a major novelist and your literary gift is rare, but you do not acknowledge it and you waste it both in elections and in dalliances."

She laughed after she emptied the cup. "Especially women. I am not saying you are a womanizer. On the contrary."

Then she looked at the young woman. "Roustum is a man who respects a woman, and he can never wrong her, or cause her any pain."

The young woman closed her lips in a long silence. She only heard the scraping of the knife in Carmen's hand on the china plate, as she cut the barbecued meat into small pieces. She took a piece onto the fork and held it without bringing it to her mouth. Her delicate fingers shook a little, the fork suspended in the air.

"Roustum is a delicate and sensitive person," she said softly, as if speaking to herself. Then she took the piece of barbecued meat into her mouth.

In the flat in al-Sayyida, Gamalat, like the police, never missed a thing. She knew more about the young woman's life than she herself did. Gamalat was frightening after she washed the make-up from her face. Her face became white and flat, like the back of her foot. The eyebrows disappeared completely, and the eyelashes, and the eyes and the lips. All her features disappeared. After she took off the veil, her hair was thin and splayed out, dyed with henna. She washed it with shampoo once a week, on that blessed Thursday night. Her hair shed with the suds and clogged the bathroom drain. She left it clogged, and the young woman cleared it, cursing her.

"May God curse your veil, Gamalat."

"What's wrong with the veil, you barefaced infidel?"

"It makes your hair fall out—it blocks the sun and air."

"Where is this air? Do you mean the dust, despair, and the despot's speeches?"

"Keep quiet, Gamalat, the walls have ears."

"What ears, my dear? Even if they have fangs, what more can they do to us?"

Gamalat laughed in her loud joyous voice. She seemed to be happy; she seemed not to know anything but happiness except for the few moments when her eyes would suddenly fill with sadness as she outlined them with her black pencil, or when she shaved her underarms and legs or when she held the thread to remove the hair from her eyebrows. Her facial muscles convulsed with pain. She remembered her mother who had killed herself in the bathroom. She sighed deeply and pointed with her finger to her head.

"My poor dead mother lost her mind when my father married another woman. He was a faithful, virtuous man. God allowed him to marry four times. My mother considered it a great betrayal. I ask for your forgiveness, God. My mother lost faith and committed suicide. My father died one week after her, from grief."

She laughed until her eyes teared. Her voice

trembled with sobbing that made her plump body shake. Her breathing was uneven and her voice cracked.

"My father was never faithful to my mother, except after she died. May God forgive him and be kind to him... O God."

Gamalat took half the young woman's wages for the rent of the room. She added to that the cost of electricity, water, and gas. What was left was barely enough for the young woman's three meals: a cup of tea and half a loaf of bread with white cheese for breakfast, half a loaf of bread with eggs and green olives for lunch without a cup of tea or with one that Mohammed the waiter in the club brought to her, and a whole loaf of bread filled with fava beans or falafel for dinner. Gamalat got to know all the people the young woman knew. She had her own way of entering deeply into her life. She smelled love relationships before they took place. She came into her room and dipped her nose in the pillow.

"Samih was with you yesterday?"

She had a strong sense of smell. Her black, thick, snub nose trembled, almost like the nose of a police dog. She read the Yassin passage from the Quran atop the young woman's bed, to expel non-Muslim devils. She said that her own devil was a Muslim just like the Prophet Mohammed's, may prayer and peace be upon him, and she repeated the Hadith to that effect. She looked into the young woman's handbag and asked her if she had a ten- or twenty-pound note. When she found none she sucked her lips.

"Aren't you able to get something from Samih or Roustum? I mean a loan to be paid back, like the loans of the World Bank, or a donation that's not to be returned, like the ones from the Americans!"

She let out her loud joyful laugh. The young woman sometimes got angry and banished her from the room, but eventually she got used to her sense of humor. Gamalat used to say she had an innocent Islamic sense of humor, just as she slaughtered according to Islamic custom. She slaughtered chickens in the kitchen sink, saying "There's no God but Allah" and severing their heads without a blink. She would then place the chicken in boiling water and pluck its feathers with strong and firm fingers, just as she plucked her eyebrows and the hair from her upper lip.

Gamalat used to accept presents from her male friends, or long-term loans.

"The Prophet accepted gifts, my dear."

Samih wanted the young woman to leave Gamalat's and live with him in his flat overlooking the Nile. It was spacious and consisted of seven rooms and three bathrooms. He lived there alone after he separated from Susan. She was a visual artist and had held many exhibitions at home and abroad. Her great-grandfather was a pasha during the monarchy. He had owned land and property. His property was sequestered by the government and transferred to the office of the president. He died of a brain hemorrhage. Her mother and father lived in poverty. Susan had rebelled since childhood through drawing. She became famous when she was a student at the Arts Institute. Samih met her at one of her exhibitions. He pulled her into Dar al-Nashr to design his book covers and she pulled him into bed in her flat in al-Mohandeseen. She became part of the elite, wading in parties and in cultural festivities. The blood of pashas flowed in her veins. Among the elites, she became famous as Madam Suzy.

Suzy, like Samih, did not believe in the marriage law. She called it a regressive law, from the times of slavery. Love united them, without a certificate. Their love began steamy and hot and ended cold and frigid. Each of them started looking for something new or for a beating under the ribs.

هههه

Gamalat pointed her finger to her left breast directly above the heart.

"The pain pricks here like a needle."

The young woman thought that this concerned a new love but the doctor decided to admit her to the hospital to carry out tests and x-rays. A malignant tumor was growing in her breast. Gamalat cried night and day. The young woman tried to comfort her.

"God Almighty knows better than the doctors, Gamalat. He is able to do anything and can summon something from nothing. You are a believer. You wear the veil and you constantly pray and fast. God will not let you down, Gamalat, and He will command the tumor to turn out benign."

She dried her tears and smiled helplessly.

"Your words make me regain my trust in God. I lost trust in Him. How could He afflict me with this disease? If this is a test, God, then it is a difficult one. More difficult than the high-school exam. I used to absolutely hate school. I've hated reading and writing all my life. I was careless and I committed many sins, but God, you are forgiving and merciful. You forgive all sins except polytheism, and God, I have never believed in any God but you. I beg for God Almighty's forgiveness for every mighty misdeed. It seems that I disbelieved in You, God of the universe, the most merciful of all. Forgive me, God and drive the devil and the malignant disease away from me."

Gamalat came out of the hospital after a few days as if she were newly born. The young woman was reading in her room when she heard the front door open. She saw Gamalat in front of her, beaming with joy. She embraced her.

"God is great—He heard my prayer and the tumor turned out to be benign, thank God."

Then her look of joy disappeared. "I paid a thousand pounds to the hospital and I still have a thousand outstanding. Two thousand pounds, God, merely for some tests! From where shall I get the other thousand, God?"

"God is generous, Gamalat."

"Yes, God is generous with everything, my dear, except with money!"

"May Almighty God forgive you."

"Don't talk too much. Heaven does not rain down pounds. Go to Samih or Roustum and borrow a thousand pounds."

"I have never borrowed from anyone. I would rather go hungry than borrow from anyone, especially from Samih or Roustum."

"Borrowing is not forbidden—God allows taking loans!"

Gamalat did not stop insisting until the young woman asked for a thousand pounds from Samih. Samih was closer to her. Her relationship with Roustum was still oscillating with their contradictory love, back and forth between separation and reconciliation, the swelling of pride and the shrinking of will, the attempt at freedom and the surrender to desire, oscillating waves of pain and joy, shame and sin.

Her relationship with Samih was quiet and cold. It was devoid of wild emotions, an established and settled marriage. Samih gave her the thousand pounds casually, as if it were an ordinary thing. She did not open the envelope. She hid it in her bag as if it were some kind of abomination. As soon as she went home she rid herself of it. Gamalat opened the envelope with strong and firm fingers. She counted the thousand pounds. Not a penny was missing. She put them in her handbag.

"I wish I had asked for a thousand five hundred!"

⁕

The villa in Garden City was filled with guests and visitors. Lights sparkled from one hall to another and faces beamed with happiness. Laughter rose with swirls of cigarette smoke and amused chortles, soft voices with the scent of jasmine and feminine perfumes and eau de cologne. Carmen swam in that atmosphere like a silver fish. Roustum sipped wine and wandered away as usual and Samih was immersed in conversation in a corner of the room. Gamalat and Miriam the poet stood on the balcony overlooking the Nile and whispered. The young woman sat alone as usual and felt estranged. She walked to the entrance of the big library and looked at the rows of books. She busied herself reading the titles. Roustum came up and walked beside her with the glass of wine in his left hand and a cigar between his lips.

"Do you always run away like this?"

He talked to her without looking at her as he inhaled the smoke. His eyes wandered over the books and stopped at a particular title. He pulled out the book and handed it to her: "This is a beautiful novel. I would love to discuss it with you after you have read it."

She glimpsed Carmen looking at her out of the corner of her eye. Her laughter rose in the air, joyful and polished like a silver container. She was absorbed in argument with some of the guests and Roustum was absorbed in surveying the rows of books and talking to the young woman without looking in her direction.

"What do you say to having dinner together and discussing the novel next Thursday?"

"Pardon?"

"Are you busy?"

"With many things."

The smell of the barbecue became stronger and voices were raised, calling them to dinner. Carmen sat at the head of the table and Roustum opened bottles of wine. Gamalat asked for fruit juice because God forbade alcohol and eating pork.

"Your friend has a sense of humor," Samih whispered in her ear.

The music had a beautiful melody she did not know. Tchaikovsky, Carmen said. She shook her head and looked from face to face. Her eyes met Roustum's. He smiled and raised his cup toward her.

"To your health."

After a while, the glow of these parties began to fade. The young woman started to feel bored and estranged. She did not belong to this milieu, although she sometimes yearned for the conversations that took place here. She accepted Roustum's dinner invitation. Her pleasure at talking about the novel with him seemed sinful.

They walked together in the dark and entered the house that was far away in the desert. Roustum took off his mask, his tie, and his shoes and walked barefoot on the sand. They played like children.

"The wolf has gone round and round with seven wraps round his tail."

He embraced her under the moon, gazing at the sky with his eyes.

"I am sick of my life full of hypocrisy. Please take me."

He was the one saying *take me*, as if she were the man and he the woman. He became another person in her arms, someone she barely knew. He extinguished his fire in her body. Never in her life had she practiced taking a man. Her experience in love was singular: the man took the woman, and not the other way around. He taught her new things, opened her eyes to things she did not know, novels she had not read, music she had not heard. Life began to seem richer to her, with many colors, such as those of birds and wildflowers in jungles that grow alone and climb freely without fences.

In the club's library she spent the day reading. If she got bored or tired she went out for a little walk in the children's garden. She made small conversation with a servant or a nanny they called "Dada Magda," who only knew a few words of Arabic. She sat beside her on the ground near the sand playground. (She was not allowed to sit on the chairs that the members sat on.) They became friends. Magda was short for Magdalene. She was born in a village near Lahore of a Muslim Pakistani father and a Hindu mother. She was raped by her father's cousin when she was eleven. Her belly swelled and she ran away before her father killed her. She rode the train in the darkness of night to Lahore. She got rid of the baby and her name became Magdalene instead of Khadiga. She omitted her father's name. The owner of an employment office told her to take her mother's name, Fofo. She sent the office half her wages every month, according to the contract.

Magda did not stop talking. She had a store of tales inside her. Her eyes were black and wide. They had an appealing luster, a mixture of Asian, Arabic, Islamic, and Hindu blood, and a hint of beautiful sadness. She had a wide imagination, as she had traveled to many countries of the world, from the slave markets of Lahore to Manila, from Riyadh to Mecca and Israel, from London, Paris, and New York to Beirut and Cairo. She knew the secrets of palaces and houses. She went to bed with ministers, ambassadors, servants, cooks, and garbage collectors. She told stories about the club members as she sat in the sand. She watched the two children attentively while she talked. Their father was an important person in the Shura Council. He shared her bed when his wife was traveling. He was an old man trying to remain youthful. He dyed his hair and moustache with black henna from Baghdad. He swallowed blue Viagra pills. She often saw his picture on the

119

front page with the president. By his first wife, he had a son who was an expert in the stock market, and from his second wife, a son who was a businessman who had partnerships with the sons of presidents of big corporations. As for his third wife, she was a relative of the Shura Council's secretary, who monitored the candidates and the election results. No one won without his efforts. He had been penniless but was now a millionaire.

Magda used to regale her with stories and pieces of Black Forest gâteau, dried fruit, hazelnuts, pistachios, and other things, which she considered to be compensation for her stolen liberty. She laughed as she shook her long, black silky hair. It was the surcharge for free love when the lady of the house was absent. She spoke in a mixture of Arabic, English, and Urdu, and then she would rise and brush the sand from her clothes and take the two children by the hand. They tried to break loose from her iron grip. Her eyes filled with hate as she looked at them. She slapped one of them on the back of his neck and punched the other on his shoulder and then she pulled them behind her like two rabbits, by the ears.

بسم

It was a warm summer night. Roustum was driving his Mercedes. The moon was hidden behind a transparent veil. The young woman filled her lungs with the desert night air. It was dry and soft, like silk. It filled her with a longing for something unknown. He stopped the car in front of the little house. They sat on the sand and drank cold beer with pieces of fresh cucumber and green olives. He drifted away and she was silent. She watched the sky as the white beams disappeared behind a cloud. The face of the moon was made of silver, shining in the darkness, with a cunning smile that kept the god hidden. He was disguised in the form of a moon. The moon radiated in the sky, then came down to the belly of the earth to become the god of death. She remembered her dead mother. Everything is fated to die, even her. Her mind was unable to comprehend the idea that she would perish the same as the ant crawling across the sand in front of her. She also could not believe in rebirth or in life after death. She was overcome by a violent desire to be embraced and drowned by him in love, before she died.

"Do you ever think of writing a novel?"

The question surprised her. His voice was hoarse and rattled, as if he were suffering from chest pain or a sore throat. She only shook her head. She had never thought of writing a novel, or anything else. Maybe the idea had occurred to her when she was fast asleep or in the depths of childhood before she became aware. It was a mysterious idea that slipped out from behind a black cloud. The idea scared her, like death.

She heard him sigh, making a small moaning sound.

"Oh, writing is hell itself. It has tortured me all my life. My imagination is impotent and cold, considering the heat of events. Every day there is an important political event, and preoccupations with the Council, and the elections. Writing requires constancy, toil, starvation, and suffering. I am satiated and spent, every inch of me. What does writing do? It is only words on paper, a release of suppressed anger, like masturbation."

The word *masturbation* rang sharply in her ear. She was not accustomed to listening to words like these coming from him, words that were considered impolite.

"I am sorry if I have hurt your feelings."

He said it as he brought his body closer to hers. He clung to her like a drowning person clings to a rescue boat. He was panting and his words came out broken and incomplete from his lips.

"Some... sometimes... I en... en... envy you.

"Why?"

"Because you are happy."

"Me?"

"At... least... you're not burdened... not burdened... with... with... writing."

His fingers trembled and were icy cold. His eyes widened and looked off. The faint light of the moon was reflected in them. His lips parted in a weak smile.

"I am tired... I am not... I am not made for writing. In reality... in reality... I am not... gifted. They made me into a big writer by inheritance... by intermediaries... with money... and dinner parties and alcohol and women...."

The word *women* rang sharply in her ears. She had not heard that tone from him before, that cheapness, that lack of respect. And she was one of them. He encircled her in his arms and tried to press his cold lips on her hot face. The cold ran through her body like a tremor. She pushed him away from her. He pulled her forcefully toward him. He tried to rape her, with force and cruelty, as if he were releasing his suppressed anger into her body. She slipped from his grasp. She had lost her appetite for love. She swallowed the bitterness and the feeling of humiliation. She remembered Carmen telling her that Roustum was weak, contradictory, a big baby looking for his mother's breast. "He fails to love a woman," she said, "so what can you expect from his writing?"

It was a failed attempt to penetrate her body. Her mind was alert and wary, blocking his way. The young woman whispered, choking.

"You are a child, Roustum."

"All men are children in a woman's arms."

"Please don't talk like Samih."

"Please don't talk like Carmen."

"Carmen is a gifted writer."

"Am I not gifted?"

"In politics."

"And in writing?"

"No, Roustum."

He held her body with angry violence, with the violence of love, as if love and anger were two aspects of the same thing, as if love drew to it anger, envy, jealousy, desperation, and sorrow inherited from childhood. As if love were not between two people, him and her, but between four people, Carmen, Roustum, Samih, and her. Imposed on the four of them were four others, each of their pictures of themselves, and then also a picture each of them had of another. Sixteen people. And each of these with a double face. All the faces appeared before her as he covered her. His lips were cold, but his breath was hot. It brushed her neck with the dry breeze of the desert night. He whispered in her ear, but his words sounded as though they were coming from a faraway place.

"I love you. I love you, forever."

The word *forever* rang in a space as empty as the desert. It echoed in her ear. She remembered Miriam the poet who sang her poem on the bank of the Nile under the light of the moon.

> What is the meaning of forever?
> Do we live forever and not die?
> And if we live, then for how long?
> Fifty, seventy, a hundred years?
> Age is not measured by years—
> A moment of love under the moon
> is worth a thousand years.

The light of the moon slipped under her light dress to her body. She lay on the sand looking at the sky. She watched the moon disappear behind a cloud, and the god with it. Beside her lay the body of a person she did not know. Was he Roustum? Or one of the sixteen? He was naked as the day his mother gave birth to him. Drops of sweat shone on his back under the light of the moon, like pearls. Miriam's voice persisted.

A moment of love under the moon
is worth a thousand years
and the sweetest love is the most untruthful,
like poetry.

Miriam used to say that love was like poetry: beyond truth and lies. There was no virtue or vice in poetry or love, no good or evil, no god or devil. If God wanted to descend to earth he would be a poet drowned in love like al-Qays, who was crazed by Layla. Samih contradicted her and said that if God wanted to come down to earth he should come as Gandhi said, in the form of a loaf of bread, or millions of people would turn away from him. And as for Carmen, she would say that if there were a God in heaven, then children would not starve to death or die in wars. Roustum smiled wearily.

"I wish God would come down as a prosecutor to arrest those in power and the members of the Shura Council."

In the wide hall Miriam recited her poem. Thousands of eyes looked at her. She sang of love like a true diva of the east. Their hearts beat with the pulse in her veins and their hands swelled from clapping. The bodies of men and women shook with intoxication. They took off everything from their heads: fezzes, hats, veils, bands, caps from Mecca, white turbans of sheikhs, and black ones of priests.

Miriam glowed under the lights. She wore her green dress decorated with white jasmine flowers. A pearl ornamented her thick black hair. A long jasmine necklace hung from her neck. Men and women competed for her love. She renounced everything but poetry. She was immune to any temptation from any party. She refused membership in the Shura Council and the Higher Council for Poets, and the President's prizes. The people looked at her like a star in the sky, difficult to attain and impossible to possess.

Gamalat looked at her enviously, and told her she was an infidel who would eventually go to hell.

Miriam laughed. "And what about you, Gamalat, what are you fated for?"

Gamalat asserted that she would go to Paradise and be there for eternity.

The young woman pursed her lips when she heard the world *eternity*. The three women were sitting in the ship's casino on the Nile. Miriam sipped wine and ate peanuts. Tears trapped in her eyes shone in the moonlight. She thought of herself as a child. Miriam had been ten years old when she opened her eyes in the dark and saw her mother standing upright in her black dress. She only wore that dress during catastrophes.

After her fourth glass of wine Gamalat asked, "What kind of catastrophes, Miriam, occurred in your mother's life?"

"For instance, the death of her mother, my granny, and her sister, my aunt, committing suicide, and her father, my grandfather, going to jail, or the start of war, or a fierce quarrel between her and her husband."

With a heavy tongue and a mind half absent, Gamalat asked, "Your mother's husband was your father?"

"Yes, and he used to quarrel with my mother over the smallest things. If she looked from the window, if she sighed or forgot and drew the cross over her chest. She was a Copt and he was a Muslim. They had a big quarrel on the day I was born. My father insisted on calling me Khadija, the mother of the faithful, and my mother insisted on calling me Miriam, after the Virgin Mary. Their quarrel continued for six days and on the seventh day they ceased temporarily and made a deal: my father would name the boys and my mother would name the girls. My father thought he came out of the battle victorious, because to God a boy is more important than a girl, according to the verse in the Quran that says 'and a male is unlike a female.' And my mother thought she'd won because Miriam has a whole chapter in the Quran. Out of all the women in the world, God mentioned only her in the Quran by name. Even Khadija, the mother of the faithful, was not mentioned in a single verse."

The other half of Gamalat's mind had gone absent by her ninth or tenth glass. Her laughter sparkled like silver. Miriam shared her laugher, with her head raised high with confidence. Beside her the young woman sat shrunken and sad. She did not have a mother and a father to quarrel over her name. No one mentioned her name. She herself had forgotten it until she heard the doctor in Barcelona calling her Nouria. The name rang beautifully in her ear. *Nouria* is a rare name, like a raindrop in the desert. The doctor asked her for her daughter's name.

"My daughter will carry my name, just as Zapatero carries his mother's name."

❧

In Barcelona, flowers bloom in spring. The weather changes with the seasons. Leaves fall from the trees in autumn. Before they fall, they take on all sorts of colors: red, yellow, green, orange, gold, silver, emerald, ruby, and coral. Red explodes, dominating the other colors, turning the sky blood red. The ground becomes a rainbow of color.

The young woman stepped on the leaves as she walked. The colored leaves moved under her feet like living creatures. They twisted, bent, rose, and brightly shone under the rays of the sun, covered with dew and a light drizzle.

Yolanda snatched the child from her arms. The child's features resembled those of her absent son, Francisco. Lab tests and DNA can prove blood relationships. Yolanda breastfed her. She placed her black nipple in her mouth. Milk flowed like a river, the kind of rushing waterfall that could bring down dams. Yolanda changed. Her youth returned with her motherly instinct. There was nothing else in her life except that little girl named Nouria, the name of her mother and her grandmother. Yolanda recalled her own mother's and grandmother's faces. She looked at Nouria and saw her absent son and her emigrant daughter and all her sons and daughters scattered among the countries of the world.

"I will give you half the restaurant and the flat in the building and take Nouria."

"Listen, Yolanda, my daughter is not for sale!"

"I will give you thirty thousand euros cash."

"My daughter is not for sale."

"She is not only your daughter. My son Francisco is her father."

"She has no father, not Francisco or anyone else. I am the mother and I decide who the father is!"

෴

Gamalat did not like the spring in Cairo. She called it the season of the khamsin winds and sandstorms. The wind came in from the desert laden with sand and the universe looked yellow.

Her eyes got inflamed and red.

She wore black sunglasses and everything she saw was black. She cursed the world, religion, everything, including herself.

"I am a hypocrite, like everyone else. I have to lie in order to live. I have to write my weekly column. I have to say things that depend on the prevailing atmosphere and the atmosphere in our country is contaminated with poisons, dust, and smoke. Even spring, the season of love, of flowers and joy in the world, is the season of disgust, pitch, and tar for us!"

Then she would burst out crying and laughing. Her red eyes teared up and she wiped them with a tissue. She pulled them out of the rectangular box with the word *Kleenex* printed in foreign letters. Her amputated laugh turned into a broken sob. Her voice rattled and came out of her nose, which dripped like a faucet. She wiped it with tissues, which filled the wastebasket.

"The flu comes even in the spring, along with the C virus, the Mediterranean virus, and the grand agenda for the Middle East. Even the tissue we use to wipe our noses we are unable to manufacture. We import them with foreign currency from the USA, along with wheat, bread, and beans. May God destroy your home, you despot, and may he destroy the home of your friend in the White House!"

The doorbell rang. Some of Gamalat's friends and colleagues in the press came to visit. Among them was Bahy al-Din Boram, who carried a bundle of roses wrapped in clear plastic. He held out a new book of literary criticism he had written. It had a whole chapter on Gamalat, the impressive writer. He sat next to her bed and read the chapter's introduction to her.

"The writer Gamalat is different from other female writers, as she does not write about sex or female bodily desires. She has a refined and balanced literary style and is keen on morality, the family, and religious values. She always directs herself toward God, the Creator of the universe, in her weekly column, and to the beloved President, who is the protector of the homeland, and to the First Lady, who is the emancipator of women and the guardian of culture, reformation, and enlightenment."

Gamalat slapped her cheeks with her hands and screamed. Flu and headache blocked her nose and ears. One word rang in her head: *forgery*.* "Your day will be a black one, Bahy Boram. Do you want to get me in trouble?"

Gamalat did not relent until he handed her the book. She put on her gold-framed reading glasses. She wanted to see that the word was *enlightenment* and not *forgery*. She slid the book under her pillow and color returned to her pale face and playfulness came back into her voice.

---

* "Enlightenment" in Arabic is *tanuleer*; "forgery" is *tanzeer*.

131

"The Arabic language is dangerous. One small dot of a letter can get you put in prison and this is one hundred percent a deliberate misprint. The workers in the press have become followers of the Arab Afghans, al-Qaeda, and Osama bin Laden. They want to insult the authorities in my name and yours, Bahy. They are hypocrites, cowards, and agents of the editor-in-chief. The whole universe is upside down, and I am sick and my head hurts!"

Samih could see the light in the young woman's room from the street. She was trying to write, and was reading a novel. He went to visit her carrying a bag of oranges or bananas or a bundle of papers and black pens. He encouraged her to write. He took her to Alexandria in the summer. He had inherited from his mother a flat overlooking the sea at Sidi Bishr. He taught her to swim. The waves seemed just as scary as writing. She tried to overcome her fear, but she did not know how to float. Late at night the page faced her, white and looming like a cloud.

She walked with Samih on the shore. The air was pure and the night quiet after people had gone to sleep. They walked until the morning star appeared. Sometimes the waves rose high and became frightful at night, like mountains of black sand. Their roars echoed and shook the sky like the shouts of street demonstrations in al-Tahrir Square. Samih held her in his arms like a kind mother, his fingers gently touching her face. She rested her head on his shoulder and fell into a deep sleep. As soon as she opened her eyes in the dark she reached out with her hand to touch his. She wanted to make sure that he was real and not a conjuring of her imagination. In the morning after breakfast he carefully prepared tea and toast with orange or strawberry jam, skim milk, and eggs boiled for four minutes. Life seemed stable, subject to an established order. She closed her eyes in relaxation. She wished that this safe life would continue forever, that she would have four children by him, two boys and two girls. She wanted to tell him everything inside her, of her love for Roustum, as if her love for Roustum was something outside of her real life, a story or a novel written on paper that she might narrate to Samih and be done with it.

Samih was a wall she leaned against. He protected her from loneliness, sadness, and poverty. During the holidays he took her out to the gardens, for Easter and the big and small festivals. They walked in the garden at the zoo, in the Orman gardens. He held her hand in the middle of the crowd. He was so close to her that they touched. She and he were alone in the big universe. He bought her white pumpkin seeds and peanuts on the banks of the Nile and they walked long distances without feeling tired or noticing the time passing. They sat on wooden benches and ate the pumpkin seeds. A begging girl walked in front of them. Samih handed her a coin and she prayed to God to protect them from evil people. The shoeshine boy approached. Samih gave him another coin, but pulled his feet away. He was embarrassed by the idea of someone cleaning someone else's shoes. She remembered a poem by Miriam the poet.

The woman leader announced with pride that she shines her husband's shoes every morning, that she bows down to him every night after evening prayer,
for a husband comes next after the god of the heavens.
And the Prophet, peace be upon him, said,
If I were to order anyone to bow down to anyone other than God,
I would order a woman to bow down to her husband.

Miriam's poems were banned by order of the permanent high committee in al-Azhar. The memorandum that banned her work stated that the poet had transgressed the limits of sharia and encouraged women to be disobedient. The decision endured as ink on paper. But the masses long for what is forbidden; they rush to what is prohibited. The injunctions that are passed to ban dancing, singing, and drinking only lead to more dancing, singing, and drinking. Gamalat raised her ringing laugh as she emptied her glass.

"Treat me to the cause of the ailment, Bahy Boram, the most glorious of God's creatures. Quench my thirst with what God gave us, until we hear the cock's call for dawn prayer, for alcohol is not forbidden, it is only hated, and I hate it and love it, just like you, Bahy. Is there love without hate, night without day, heaven without hell?"

Roustum had asked the young woman more than once, "Do you ever think of writing a novel?"

She asked him what concern it was of his if an unknown woman like her wrote a novel. If she were to write it, would anyone read it? When she sat alone in the library, she looked at the books from the ceiling to the floor, hundreds of books. None of the club members used the library. As she walked in the streets she saw hundreds of books spread over the pavement, thousands of books, millions of books in shops, on sidewalks, in alleys. People passed them by. They lined up in front of the bakery, jostling for place in line. Then they'd emerge with creased clothes, dusty faces, sweaty, cursing the world and religion, but with a black plastic bag filled with loaves of bread.

The young woman told herself at night, I will write a novel when I wake up.

In the morning she kept her lips closed; she was unable to utter the word: *novel*. It was a secret she could not reveal to anyone, not even to herself, except in the somnolence of dreams, as if it were a private part of the body that needed to be hidden, or the small hole in the bottom of her old pair of shoes.

At Dar al-Nashr during seminars the young woman would sit between Roustum and Samih. Roustum appeared more radiant and less pale than Samih. Samih moved close to her and held her hand. His fingers were thin and delicate. She yearned for his arms and kindness. When she saw him sitting behind his huge desk her heart filled with pity for him. A prisoner between walls, he revised accounts and numbers. Roustum seemed far away, under a spotlight, like the hero of a novel she'd read long ago.

At night she contemplated Samih's pale face. He looked sad while he slept. She kissed him on the cheek, until he opened his eyes. He told her about his childhood and the dreams of his life. He'd have been a big writer like Roustum, if he had time, but he was exhausted by Dar al-Nashr. He hated the calculations of gains and losses. He wished to shut it down forever but he did not have the courage, like a husband who lived with his wife wanting to leave her but lacking the will. He was an addict.

He whispered in her ear while he cradled her in bed. "You deserve a better man than me."

"Who would that be?"

"I don't know."

"Maybe he doesn't exist."

"Maybe."

His sad eyes looked away. She lay beside him,

feeling as though she were drowning in the silence and sweat of the summer nights. She lit a Cleopatra cigarette with a match. She'd stolen it from the stash in Gamalat's room. She loved smoking. She blew the smoke from her nose and mouth, toward the ceiling. Samih disliked the smell of cigarettes, especially the Cleopatra brand. It reminded him of Gamalat. He pulled the cigarette from between her lips. He carried her to the bathroom, scrubbed her back with soap and a sponge and splashed her with water, and they laughed like children. They had played on the seashore during the summer holiday.

"What would you think of living together in my flat?"

"Under one roof?"

"Yes."

"Forever?"

"Yes."

"Impossible."

"Why?"

"I don't know."

After Samih left, the young woman lay down with a white towel wrapped around her. She buried her face in the pillow he'd slept on and breathed the smell of his hair and his breath. She longed for his body once more. She longed for him more in his absence than in his presence. The moments with him seemed gone from her life. They slipped between her fingers like a fish in water; they dissolved in her memory as salt melts in the sea.

Carmen's voice came back to her.

"A woman can never live under the same roof with a man, but what about a woman writer?"

The question turned over in her head: What is the difference between a woman and a woman writer? Does writing change a person's definition?

The young woman's resources did not allow her to live alone. Yet her life under the same roof with Gamalat disturbed her. Gamalat never stopped making noises in her bedroom, the living room, the bathroom. Maybe Gamalat was the reason she was unable to write. When she saw her face in the mornings, without eyebrows, she was frightened. But the idea of living with a husband forever frightened her more. She had never known a happy couple. Roustum said that marriage is an institution of misery and Carmen said that a happy marriage only continues out of habit or laziness. Roustum and Carmen competed for the young woman's heart. The young woman was equally attracted to each of them. Each revealed the other's faults. She listened to them as a daughter listens to her father's complaints about his wife, and her mother's complaints about her husband. She kept their secrets, and never revealed the other's complaints to either one. She had no doubt that they made up after their spats, and that she alone was the victim.

Roustum placed his head on her breast. He was thirty years older than her. She was the same age as his son, Mohammed Idris. She knew nothing about that son because he had forgotten him, willingly and unwillingly. She heard his moans as he slept beside her. He shook the past from memory, buried his face between her breasts, and poured his old sorrows into her body. He whispered in her ear with his hoarse voice.

"The past is dead and the future does not exist. This present moment is our only life, all we possess. We have to enjoy it until we lose consciousness."

He forgot her name the minute he lost consciousness. He called her Carmen. Sometimes he called her Karima, the heroine of his first novel. He had been a young man when he decided the girl of his dreams was the daughter of his uncle the pasha. He planned to marry her when he graduated from the university. He waited two years for her, on fire. He clutched her body at night. He could not see her face in the dark. He did not want to see her face. They embraced stealthily, unconsciously, averting their eyes. He did not have the courage to look into her eyes. Or she was one of the servants in the house, a poor girl from the countryside who did not know how to read or write. She called him Master Roustum as she lay under him. Her eyes were closed. She did not have the courage to open them and look into his eyes. His hot breath fell on her face and his voice rattled like the groans of a sick animal. He was cured by secreting his poison in her and pouring moans over her body. He quickly got up, regaining his strength and former status.

There was not one, two, or three victims, but more, before he got his high-school degree. His aunt used to turn away the servants one after the other. Each of them disappeared into the darkness of life and the afterlife. No one knew their fates. This one might become a belly dancer in one of the clubs or a bed servant for one of the elderly or a prostitute. That one might return to her parents who would wash away their shame with her blood or she might ride the sea with migrating birds to another shore.

One of them was more naïve than the rest. She was fifteen, an innocent child from the country-side. When Roustum visited her at night she thought him a god and herself the pure virgin. She carried his sacred semen in her womb and she did not lose her innocence until after she gave birth to the child. She carried him on her chest and went to tell her master the news. He threw her out of the palace in Garden City, she and her son. She was shocked and her heart stopped. She died, leaving the child in God's care. He started to spend day and night on the pavements under the dome of the sky, without shelter or food. Like all children of the street, he started stealing to eat, and taking drugs in order to forget. Only his father's name and address remained in his memory. His mother had told him the truth before she died. When he came of age, he went to his father. The guards prevented him from entering. One of them hit him on the back of his neck, another hit him in his belly. He fell to the floor. He was surrounded by the guards, the cook, the servants. Policemen came and carried him to the police station. He cursed life and religion and cursed his father and the grandmother who'd given birth to him. The policemen hit him and put him in jail.

"What's your name, boy?"

"Mohammed Idris, the son of Roustum Pasha."

"Shut up, you son of a prostitute."

"My mother is noble and my father is the prostitute."

The masculine form of *prostitute* was not familiar in Arabic, as the word is originally feminine and has no masculine equivalent. The story spread in the city. The opposition held on to it to use against Roustum in the Shura Council. Elections were drawing near and the scandals involving the male and female candidates preceded them. Circulars from unknown sources were brought out, intoning *karmout* rhyming with *prostitute*.

Mohammed Idris was released from prison. They took him into the party that opposed his father. They brought him with them in their campaigns. He was the spitting image of his father: the face, the forehead, the eyes, the eyebrows, the nose, the lips, the frame, the voice with the hoarseness that appealed to women. The minute that Mohammed Idris appeared before the voters they shouted, "The spitting image of Roustum Pasha and his mother Karima, the daughter of the party." Thus the candidate of the opposing party could kill two birds with one stone: His first opponent, Roustum, and his other opponent, Karima, a female journalist who was Gamalat's colleague. They called her the daughter of the party, meaning in the colloquial dialect the daughter of a loose woman and, in classical Arabic, the daughter of the venerable council.

⁂

Carmen followed the campaign from a distance. She had not known that her husband had an illegitimate child. He had told her about his adventures before he married her, but not the story of Karima, who gave the child the name of her father, Idris, and added Mohammed to it, hoping that the Prophet's name would add honor and legitimacy to her child. It was no use: Mohammed Idris suffered from a lack of honor and legitimacy until he died. After the elections were over, he was hit by a car as he ran in the streets distributing newspapers and magazines. He fell under the wheels. The papers scattered all around him, blood and ink, and the echo of his voice calling, *Ahram, Akhbar, Gomhoriya*, the president's speech for Eid.

⁂

At night Roustum buried his head in Carmen's breast. He tried to forget his son's face and the glossy posters: "Vote for the *karmout* who swims with the popular current, extolling socialism and privatization, writing short stories and novels. He is extremely attractive to women, whether on the golf course or speaking on the Gulf war and the roadmap, the stock market and Israel and Mecca. He wipes away his sins in the pilgrimage season and during the month of Ramadan and gives alms by feeding the poor."

Carmen took him her arms and quieted him like a mother. She never rebuked him and he never apologized.

"Infidelity is not a betrayal, for God has created man so that one woman cannot satisfy him," he said, inside her embrace.

He never brought up God except in this circumstance, when his wife was about to hear a new story. Carmen knew when one was about to be revealed, because Roustum would appear burdened and obsessed by sin. He would deliberately provoke her, until she became upset and exploded in anger and cursed the day she had met him. At this point he would relax and fall into a deep sleep, and wake feeling light, relieved of his burden.

"Listen, Roustum," Carmen would tell him. "I'm sick of this game. You have to take responsibility for your sins and not burden me with the responsibility of purifying you of them."

He stared at her as if he were seeing her for the first time. He was horrified that she had uncovered his hidden depths. He fell into her arms as if she were a mother, buried his face in her breast and cried in his hoarse voice, "Be angry with me, Carmen. Purify me from my sins so I can love you more." And he added silently, "So I can hate you more."

She pushed him away, then pulled him toward her. She was attracted to him and repelled by him at the same time. He got out of bed and sat beside her, his cigarette smoke rising to the ceiling. Then he put on his clothes and left. He used to go meet the young woman, if he had not found another woman. If she was away or refused to meet him, he would drive his Mercedes in the streets of the city and pick up a prostitute, take her to his place in the desert and empty his anger and disgrace. He pressed his teeth into her lips until they bled, and he bit her shoulders like a rabid dog. If she moaned, he hit her in the chest or abdomen with his fist. His masculinity flared with her moans. His voice rattled as he whispered in her ear, "Take me, lioness." The woman would get on top of him and take him forcibly the way a man takes a woman. Gamalat used to say that a man never felt pleasure except with a woman who caused him pain, blurring the border between pleasure and pain. Miriam the poet used to say that a woman is like a man: she oscillates between submission and domination, except for the women who are lionesses, who have more power than the lion.

It was a rainy winter night and the alleys in al-Sayyida were small ponds. The mice and cockroaches hid inside the cracks and people had all returned to their flats by sundown. The young woman was startled from her sleep by the sound of a scream. It was after midnight and the darkness was thick. She made out Gamalat dressed, standing by her door. Her face was pale. She had no makeup on, no eyebrows. She was beating her cheeks with her two hands.

"Oh God, why? Oh God, why?"

"What happened?"

There was no time for an answer. The taxi sped off with the two of them, crossing alleys drowned in darkness and muck. The driver cursed life and religion. Gamalat was unusually silent. The young woman sat beside her, drowned in her own thoughts. The taxi stopped in one of the alleys of the necropolis at the bottom of al-Mokatam Mountain. The cab could go no farther. Gamalat got out and the young woman followed her. They waded in the mud as they went from one alley into another. Then Gamalat stopped in front of an opening in the wall. She took a handkerchief from her pocket and placed it over her nose. The smell was unbearable. It resembled the smell of barbecued meat. At the entrance a woman stood wearing a black tent-like gown. Her eyes bulged from two holes sunk in the black. A man in a long white gown stood beside her, along with three policemen. One of them stepped toward Gamalat and shone the flashlight in her face.

"Are you her mother, Mrs. Gamalat?"

"Yes."

She uttered the word *yes* as if she were taking her last breath. Her body fell to the ground. They helped her up. She moved one foot after the other as they helped her. She stopped, hesitating, to catch her breath. The young woman moved behind her as if she were in a dream. It was too dark. The only illumination was coming from the yellow cylinder of light of a small flashlight. She fell on top of a charred mass, the shape of an infant child. Beside it was another, bigger, more charred mass. The hair on its head had been burned away. Only the bones of the face remained. The bodies had been burned and then extinguished in a pool of mud and water, except for one thing that remained like a burning ember among the ashes. It was the color of blood and glowed in the dark: an open eye with no eyelash or eyelid, which stared at them without blinking.

Gamalat lay in bed night and day. She did not go out of her house and refused to meet visitors. One of her colleagues published the story under a false name, and it was quite popular and often repeated: the mother had gotten rid of her illegitimate child by placing her in front of a mosque. One of the garbage collectors had picked her up from where the girl lived among the rubbish, like a rat. The men there had climbed on top of her, before she'd become fully conscious. She became a mother when she was but a child herself. The truth frightened her to death, brought home to her through the will of God, or by the striking of a match.

Gamalat convalesced. She got out of the bed, reached under it, and drew out a bottle by the neck. She drained one glass after another. She talked to God when she was not conscious, asking him the eternal question, "Why?" But no answer ever came to her.

The young woman turned in her bed at night. Something was growing inside her. She did not know what it was or how it had slipped inside. She thought it was an illusion made by fear or else some kind of tumor, perhaps malignant. She remembered her first meeting with Samih, at Dar al-Nashr in Heliopolis. The place was filled with young people, men and women, who dreamed of writing. In the symposiums, the discussions were about the short story and the novel. The young woman was seeking knowledge. Love was not her aim. She had wanted to become more aware and for the sake of writing she sacrificed her body. Her body was diminished to allow for the satisfaction of the mind.

What Samih took to be lust for him was lust for knowledge. She threw herself into his arms, not because she was a woman, but because she was a writer. She had never written a thing in her life.

No one knew she was a writer. She herself did not know, and if she had known, she would have hid the secret deep inside, as if it were a fault.

Maybe it was Roustum who uncovered this fault for the first time. He told her as he held her in his arms, "Your mind is lit up, like my wife Carmen's. We embrace one another as a writer embraces another writer, inside our own special world, the world of words, where the pleasures of the imagination surpass those of reality."

They embraced until they reached orgasm. They held their breath at the climax. They froze in bed, without movement. Each of them feared that if they moved the flame would die.

Carmen used to say, "Roustum and I have a ruinous relationship. I will not be calm until I completely destroy him and make him into one of my novels and he will not be calm until he destroys me." Theirs was a destructive pairing undertaken for the sake of what might remain. It was an attempt to survive past death. Neither of them excavated this secret. Maybe it was about love, and not about writing. Maybe they wanted to hide in the folds of literature, to make a noble pretext for going to bed together.

Roustum knew she loved another man and Carmen knew that he loved another woman. They both suppressed their jealousy and possessiveness, in the name of freedom and variety. The inquisitive instinct often overcame them. Each of them tried to know the other's secrets, for the sake of knowledge and not out of jealousy. Roustum wanted to know who could persuade his wife better than him and she wanted to know who could better persuade her husband. Satisfying the body is much easier than satisfying the mind.

Carmen used to say that writing is a beautiful way to hide ugly things. She took revenge on her husband in her novel. She made him sleepless with jealousy, hiring spies to learn her secret life, pursuing any man she loved with a silenced handgun. Miriam the poet said that we write to express the muteness inside us, we fear what is left unsaid more than death, and we do not think of suicide except when we fail to write.

Gamalat volunteered to spy on Roustum's private life. She was amused by finding hidden crimes. "God created good and evil," she said, "and he created the devil for temptation and diversion." She laughed as she sipped her wine and added, "And God created wine for our happiness, my dear, or else Paradise would not be filled with rivers of wine."

Gamalat discovered the love stories in Roustum's life. Their heroines were unknown young women in the literary world. Each of them chased after fame through love. Roustum went from one woman to another in the same way he went from one novel to the next. He mixed dream with reality. In one of his novels his protagonist said, "I am a man like the Prophet who has the virility of fifty men, so how can I be satisfied with four women?"

Gamalat spoke about her late husband. She had caught him one night in her bed with another woman. She had clapped her cheeks and cried out, "In my bed and in my house, you traitor?" Her voice had been loud. Her husband had jumped off the woman and held a hand over her mouth.

"Be quiet, Gamalat, or the neighbors will hear you!"

"What neighbors are you talking about? How very true that betrayal is in every man's blood, just like the proverb says. The woman who trusts a man may as well trust a sieve to hold water."

When Miriam the poet heard the story, she said, "Men can never get enough of three things— money, power, and women—and women can never get enough of three things—pain, regret, and shame."

In Barcelona, the festival of love comes during spring. Annajell visited the young woman one bright day.

"A man named Jordi loves you. He saw you walking on the shore. Do you believe in love at first sight?"

"Love does not follow a general law. Every story has its own laws, and every novel has its own particular style."

"Jordi is a young man your age, and like you he tries to write, without success. He plays drums in the Ramblas in front of a restaurant and sings. Women look at him. They are attracted by art and poverty—the two are esteemed on Valentine's Day."

"What is Valentine's Day, Annajell?"

"The feast of Saint George. He was a poor young dreamer who saved a beautiful princess from the ghoul or beastly giant who fell in love with her and wanted to devour her. The young man vanquished him. He carried the princess off on his white horse and flew with her to the shores of love in Barcelona. He gave her a red rose on their wedding anniversary and she gave him a book. The princess loved reading and writing and the people of Barcelona started celebrating the day of Saint George. They call it Valentine's Day and they exchange red roses and books."

Jordi came carrying a red rose for her. He looked like the young man of her dreams when she was a child walking by the banks of the Nile.

"I am Jordi, and you are?"

"My daughter is called Nouria. Yolanda took her."

"Children in every place are born and die and are born once more. You don't need to bear offspring, like a rabbit. You need something else. Have you tried to sing, dance, sculpt, or write?"

"*Write?*"

The word rang so sharply in her ear she awakened as if from sleep. She saw him standing before her looking almost like Samih or Roustum or Francisco or another name stirring in her forgotten memory. He almost resembled Carmen, Miriam, and Gamalat. All their features combined in the new visage. He brought together femininity and masculinity. His mother was from Barcelona and his father was from Tangiers. He was tall and slim with an olive skin mixed with red, the color of the stones that divide North Africa from southern Spain at Gibraltar. He spoke Arabic and Catalan. He had studied the comparative criticism of Arabic and Catalan literature. At night he worked at the Morocca Catalana Restaurant, serving Moroccan and Catalonian dishes in a small alley off the Ramblas. Jordi told her about Ibn Battuta, Ibn Rushd, Andalusian literature, and the first novel he was writing. The young woman started to master Catalan. It was more like French than Spanish because Catalonia is closer to France than to Madrid. His olive face smiled when he saw her. She remembered the smile of Mohammed the waiter in the club. She told him, "I like your smile, Jordi. The word *somari* in Catalan means smile. It is close to *sourire*, the French. You bring hope to my life, Jordi. The word *hope* in Catalan is *espranca* and it is close to the French and Barcelona celebrates the feast of hope at the end of April after Valentine's Day."

In the celebration of the feast of hope the young woman walked by the sea with Jordi. Men, women, children, young and old people stretched on the sand under the sun. Their bare bodies shone with drops of water. Everyone became equal, regardless of age, color, sex, or nationality. The young woman stretched out on the sand and watched them from far away. Her heart filled with a mysterious sadness. She cried without tears for her dead mother, her sister who had killed herself in the bathroom, and her neighbor who wrapped herself in a black tent. She rose suddenly and shook the sand off her body. She threw herself in the sea and swam with Jordi in its depths. His arms surrounded her underwater and he asked her about the sadness in her eyes. She didn't know the answer.

"Maybe it is an old grief from childhood, maybe it is a newly regenerated longing, Jordi. In spite of the pain and sadness, I dream of going back to my family. Can the fingernail be separated from the flesh?"

༈

Jordi was swimming in front of her. The way he was beating the water with his arms reminded her of Samih. Their features were similar, their way of moving, and their delicateness. She raced him underwater with a group of other young men and women. They laughed and played in the waves. They came out of the water and brushed off the water drops under the sun. They sat in a restaurant eating barbecued filets of the fish that live among the rocks. The name of the dish meant *shining fish*. The rocks, together with the salty water, gave it strength and lightness. They sipped a Catalonian wine called Cristina Desroches Nobel Court. They exchanged red roses and books, mostly novels.

"Why red roses and books on Valentine's Day?" Jordi asked. "Is there a relationship between love and writing?"

The young woman remembered her first meeting with Roustum, at Dar al-Nashr in Heliopolis. He had sat alone, reading. His hair was thick and black with white hair interspersed. The early gray hair endowed him with some sort of magic. She was attracted by his halting steps between the bookshelves. He was wandering, sad and lonely. His head was bent down by heavy ideas. He was neither Roustum the member of the Shura Council, nor the husband and businessman. He was another person among the others who inhabited his body. He seemed to her a soul floating among the books. She did not have the courage to speak to him, since she was an unknown young woman without a father or a mother.

Samih was not like Roustum. He understood her more. He knew that in her depths there was a longing for something bigger than love. Not the love between men and women. Something else was imprisoned inside her that did not come out into the everyday world.

"You are searching for yourself in love, for the meaning of your life, for eternal wisdom, or what people call God." Samih said. "This is the natural search that every human being undertakes with or without explicit consciousness. You don't fall in love for the sake of sex. You have sex for the sake of something else. Your aim is not to have children, but is a matter connected to writing—"

"Writing?

"Or some other thing, you know better than I. A man can never fill your imagination or satisfy your mind, or even your body. Maybe that is why love cannot transform you into a wife, a servant, or a slave, or something else that your logic might submit to. Your mind is the final shore where your strong feelings anchor. You have lived pain, sorrow, and poverty. You try to compensate for lost love and freedom by writing. You will immerse yourself in any experiment to the point of death for the sake of knowing. You're true only to your mind and you do not feel safe except with yourself.

"What about you, Samih?"

"I give you the love of an absent mother. With me you don't feel that you need the railings of your mind or the weapon you raise in Roustum's face. You see me as a fortress in which to seek protection from falling in love, because I am not the man of your dreams."

The young woman withdrew into a long silence. Roustum was closer to the man of her dreams than Samih. The man of a woman's dream is made up of images from films and the prevailing ideas about masculinity and virility. Her imagination was born of lust. She longed for a man who

155

would rape her. Images of submission had accumulated in her mind from childhood on, like a chronic illness.

"But I love *you*, Samih. I can give you everything, give you my whole life, die for your sake as a martyr dies for God and country."

"Love doesn't entail death for the sake of something else. We do not die for the love of God or country, but out of the fear we have of them. No one goes to war except under the power of compulsory enlistment and no one goes to the church or the mosque except out of fear of hell. Only the sons of the poor die in war. Churches and mosques are crowded only with the elderly and the sick."

In his heart Samih wondered why she was able to die for him, but not able to love him. Why did she not lust for him? Why did she desire Roustum, who had no principles or morals?

The young woman told herself that her feelings for Samih were stronger than all her other feelings. Maybe because they were connected by something other than sex. Maybe their souls, which were more noble than the body, were connected.

Carmen was the woman Roustum loved, but he was not the man she loved. She was preoccupied with another man she barely knew. She had concerns that took her away from sex, pregnancy, birth. Motherhood for her was not an instinct but an enforced decree. She had another necessary instinct that took her away from her husband. An instinct drove her to live alone, to be in her mind, and to write with a desire that superseded any other.

Roustum imagined her with other men in bed. She was not schooled to arouse men's desires. She was like a young virgin who had not lost her innocence, even while her experiences with men and women were numerous. She came out of every experience with a new sense of disappointment and another headache. The doctors failed to cure her chronic headaches and she gave in to depression as if she were giving in to love. The drawers of her desk were filled with bottles of pills, as was her dresser and the table beside her bed. Pills for headaches and depression surrounded her along with books, papers, and pens. She took protection in them from the noise, the newspaper headlines, the crowds, and the screaming children. She sat behind her closed double-paned window, looking at the city from far away. She saw people without anyone seeing her, like a god in the sky suffering from loneliness. She loved it and hated it at the same time. She was repelled by people and at the same time overcome by a longing for them.

At night she called out for Roustum and he came to her. As soon as she saw him, she distanced herself.

"Oh, not you."

If the other person came to her she would also say, "Not you."

She cried alone, because she was separate. She searched for love, uselessly. She was a puzzle to everyone who knew her, just like life, just like death, just like everything present and absent.

"She's a symbol for everything difficult to attain," Roustum said. "She is a symbol for something that is very far away, like a star in the sky that cannot be possessed. The more distant she is the more one longs more for her, unto death."

A heroine in a novel of Carmen's said, "Death in love is no more than an aspect of love. Love is only a symbol for something else and it is stupid for a person to die for a symbol." The word *symbol* is sacred because it contains all that people worship from birth until death, everything that children learn by heart and chant every morning in school, the Holy Trinity, the Father, the Son, and the Holy Spirit, or God, Country, and King, though the word *king* was removed after the fall of the monarchy and was replaced by the word *president*, there is always a sacred person.

The election season was approaching. The story of the illegitimate child was not even forgotten before Roustum's adversaries in the Shura Council began searching for other scandals. Several of them found a copy of a novel in his wife's handwriting. They stopped at the final sentence: "It is stupid for a person to die for a symbol." The following day circulars and fliers appeared on the walls in the streets. The wife was accused of harboring hostility for the sacred symbol and the accusation shifted to her husband, since he is responsible for his wife, as every shepherd is responsible for his flock. Roustum became the enemy of God, Country, and President.

Roustum and Carmen quarreled at home. He hammered the air with his fist in anger.

"You are the cause of all these problems. You are the reason for my failure at everything—in politics and in literature."

He had a deep wound that never healed, an old and chronic wound of which he did not know the origins. He had been struck by an arrow at their first meeting, and the pain in his chest had been pricking at him since. It would not subside until she smiled at him and confessed that she loved him.

She never confessed. Instead, she asked, "What does love mean?"

He answered by writing her a letter in which he described the stirrings of his heart. She asked him what he meant by "heart"—was it separate from the body and the mind? He answered with another letter, asking her what she meant.

"We are all sick from the dualities of body and heart, brain and spirit," Carmen said. The discussion that began on their wedding night would go on between them all their lives. Nothing would cure them of this illness except the word *love*, uttered between sips of wine on the balcony overlooking the Nile. Roustum was caught between his intellect and his feeling. He believed in a creative soul that has no body. Carmen believed that the universe has existed for millions of years, which proceed in the figure of a circle, not in a straight line.

Roustum said, "In the beginning, there was the word."

And Carmen asked, "Which word?"

"The word of God."

He confessed that while he was in her arms that thought never arose, but it had been among the deep sentiments of his childhood. Carmen asked him what he meant by "sentiment." Roustum was confused a little, then said, "Sentiment is the feeling or the void of feeling when the spirit inhabits a child's body and grows with him from birth and leaves him at death."

The disagreements between them melted in bed as they embraced. Their two bodies united. Words became meaningless. Carmen whispered at climax, "In the beginning there was the body and not the word, Roustum. I mean the complete body, the body that contains brain, soul, heart, sentiment, marrow, and bones." Roustum was exhausted by this and fell into deep sleep.

Carmen told the young woman when she visited her in the mental hospital, "What is the use of them tying me with a rope to the bedrails? What is the use of locking my novel in the closet?"

Carmen was lying in room number 1438 after the doctors directed an electric current to her brain. She did not lose her memory despite the strength of the electricity. She recognized her face in the young woman's features. The young woman resembled her daughter, who was absent from memory. She had given birth to her in a place and time she knew nothing about. She was lying alone in a room locked by iron rails resembling a prison cell. Above the bed a paper hung with the patient's name. The young woman visited her late at night. The patients were asleep and unconscious. They were drugged by the poisons injected into their bloodstream or the currents directed to their brains. The place seemed deserted. Time seemed to have ended. The whole building was drowned in the unconsciousness of sleep or death, the male and female patients, the doctors and nurses, except for her, Carmen: she was conscious and awake, waiting for the young woman. No one visited her except the young woman. Her features were like those of a child she had seen in a dream or in the mirror when she was a child. She was lying down, bound by rope. Beside her on the table was a box of medicine, sleeping pills, pills for depression, a water pitcher, food plates—everything that a human being needs, except pen and paper. An edict of accusation and condemnation had been inscribed on her forehead before she was born.

She was unable to sleep, despite the sleeping pills. She stole an hour or half an hour of sleep from the night. She opened her eyes, which had been open from birth. She lingered, abstracted in the horizon until the morning star appeared. Morning was a long burden she was forced to carry and walk with, though she lay in bed. She drove her small Fiat and roamed the city streets with the young woman beside her. They stole an hour or half an hour from time. Her husband was jealous of the young woman, as if she were a secret lover, or a pen and white sheet of paper. He got close to her, hoping to take her away from writing, but to no avail. The novel would keep chasing her until death. The room in the hospital was dark. There was a long succession of locked rooms. The wooden doors were painted white. Everything in the hospital was white, even the shroud, the bedrails, hallways, the moans heard behind walls, the sound of the doctor's heels on the floor. Roustum came to visit with the face of an angel, then disappeared into the light like a summer cloud.

Tied to the bed, Carmen said to the young woman, "Open the closet and read the novel. Writing is a ritual undertaken from birth until death, a ritual undertaken without fear, except this is impossible as we live and die in fear, in burning fire and electric shock and antidepressants. There is no deliverance, no hope, except through writing."

The young woman saw tears in her eyes. Nothing defeated her except her tears. She remained beside her frozen in silence. If she reached out her hand to touch her she would shudder and wake from her coma. Carmen smiled, realizing that she was the daughter whom she had lost. She wanted to release her from the lie of love, as if it were in her power to release her, as if she held the prison key in her hand.

The game of love exhausted Roustum, like the games of writing and politics.

"The three lack fidelity and honest intention. The ugliest thing about all three is that the faces of the players are so serious and grave. They utter grandiose words filled with the trappings of justice and liberty. Their saliva flies into the air as they pronounce them emphatically. They borrow from God's books what they want and leave out what they don't want."

They were all victims and offenders, men and women, except his wife. She was the only one, among all people, whom he loved. After he drowned her with his love he would dart off to other women, as if betrayal were no more than an assertion of love. He wanted to drink from all the cups in the world, then return to his favorite cup. She wrote her novel about him. She called him by another man's name. She created him in a form that appealed to her. His real features did not attract her, nor his novels with their shining covers and his picture displayed to the reader. She tried to be rid of him by means of another man's image. She was moved by his tears when he returned to her, repentant. He knelt between her hands, as if he were in prayer, asking for mercy and forgiveness, like a child crying in his mother's arms, like a faithful worshipper in the hands of his god. In the morning she opened her eyes to find him in her arms. His lips parted with a smile to see her, a smile unique to him alone, a smile that did not resemble any other man's smile. She realized for certain that she loved him, and that she did not love anyone else. She wanted him to get dressed and leave without returning.

"You and Carmen are opposites," Roustum told the young woman. "Nothing brings you together except the craziness of writing. Neither of your beds is big enough for a man, or even half a man—the whole space is filled with pages of a novel, broken pencils, dry tears. Each of you embraces your novel as you sleep as if it were a man you love and want to devour to the marrow, give birth to his child, and then throw him away like a drained stalk of sugar cane."

Miriam the poet was unlike his wife. Men sensed that she was different from other women. No man could possess her, even if she were in his arms. She was not a wife, lover, whore, or saint. She was herself, Miriam the poet, and nothing else. She was the impossible and the mirage that men and women ran after. She was able to do without the things that lead to annihilation, as was al-Khansaa, or al-Zaba', the female poet. She repeated the poetry of al-Zaba', who chose poetry over earthly possessions and things treasured by people.

After I now sleep and awaken free,
    and men have no authority over me,
am I to be owned by a husband?
    That's the worst fate that may await me.
To live in injury, poverty, and need with
    dignity is better than a tongue's exchange.

Another poet, Aisha al-Kortobiya, said to a man she didn't want who wanted her:

> I am a lioness but I am not content
> > to live according to someone else's
> > inclination.
> Even if I were to choose this I would not
> > answer to
> > a dog, for I have blocked my ears to many
> > a lion.

The poet used to say that she herself was a lioness who could only accept a lion, except that she was not contented with lions.

Aisha al-Kortobiya was from Cordoba. Arab and Spanish blood ran in her veins. She lived freely and wrote poetry. The poet Afira Elshomoos was raped by the despot Amleek, so she went out among the people, cursing men without feeling ashamed.

> What happens to your women is unseemly
> > though you are as numerous as ants.
> If we were the men and you the women
> > we would not countenance such a deed.
> So die with dignity or kill your enemy
> > and give light to God's fire with ample
> > embers.
> For no good can come from permitting injury,
> > and death is better than disgrace.
> So exile and annihilation to one who provides
> > no shield and walks proudly among us
> > like a mule.

165

Miriam the poet sings the verses of al-Khansa, who refuses to get married to a man called Master of the Arabs, whom she sees as something else.

God forbids Hiraky to marry me
He is shorter than Jashm Ibn Bakr
And if I find myself with Jashm
then I am in poverty and filth.

The poet Hind, the mother of Moawiya the Caliph, participated in the wars of Quraysh waged against Prophet Mohammed, and she slit open the belly of his uncle Hamza.

I cured myself of Hamza in Uhud
when I cut his liver out of his belly.

The poet Laila al-Akhyaliya was forced to marry someone she did not desire, so she carried on loving another man called Tawba, in public and not in secret. She wrote poetry for him. Others thought him ugly, but she saw him as the most beautiful human being.

If you saw Tawba with your true eyes you
would wish
that every woman in your house would carry
his child.

The Caliph Abdul Malek Ibn Marawan asked her, "What was Tawba's opinion of you when he loved you?" She said, "The same as the people had of you when they made you king."

The poet Um al-Ward, who made fun of her husband, said, "I swear by God he will not embrace me, kiss me, or even smell me."

The poet Rabi'a El Adawiya, who was raped in the slave market when she was a child, abandoned men and their bodies and lived with poetry and her love for the symbol of justice, or God:

> I deserted human beings altogether hoping
> to unite with You, as this is my ultimate
> desire.

Miriam the poet glowed when she recited her verses and the verses of other female poets. Her long neck stretched as she stood before the microphone and shone under the lights. Men and women hated and admired her. They looked at her with envy. Her eyes passed over their heads and she rose above femininity, masculinity, and the finitude of things. They said that she had two sexes and many identities. They searched her life for something embarrassing, for a scandal that would hurt her pride. They spoke ill of her behind her back and praised her in her presence. She did not care for flattery or slander. She took her value from herself and her head did not know how to bow.

One warm evening in the desert with the young woman in his arms, Roustum said, "I want to confess something to you I have not confessed to myself."

She had never seen such tears in his eyes. His heart was filled with heavy sin. When he was ten years old he was lying in his bed with his aunt next to him. Her husband was in prison for the crime of trying to violently overthrow the regime. Her husband had never in his life carried a tool for killing. He used to carry a pen and write poems. He said in one of his verses, "We are a nation of slaves, we pursue our daily bread in his majesty's shadow, he who sits on the throne for life."

His aunt whispered in his ear, "Roustum, you are beautiful."

His mother was not in the house. His father said that she had left him for another man and his aunt said that the opposite was true. His father divorced his mother because of another woman. Roustum never found out the truth. His aunt surrounded him with her kind arms. He wept upon her breast for his absent mother and she wept upon his for her imprisoned husband. She brushed away his tears with her lips as she kissed him on his cheeks. Her lips went lower to his mouth as she covered it and whispered, "Roustum, you are beautiful." He would sleep on top of her breasts as she sang lullabies to him. He closed his eyes, pretending to sleep, and submitted to her arms, feeling the pleasure of one body touching another. He realized in a mysterious way that she was of another sex. Maybe she was the female and he was the male, maybe their pleasure was a sin that would be punished in hell after death. But the idea of death never even preoccupied him as a child, so why worry about a hell that comes *after* death? He slept in her arms until morning. She prepared breakfast for him. He drank the milk with his head bent. He never had the courage to look into her eyes. He saw her as the devil who brought Adam down from Heaven. At night she appeared to him like a pure angel. Warmth passed from her body to his. She whispered in his ear, "Roustum, you are beautiful and God loves beauty." Pleasure got mixed with beauty, God, and his aunt. She died one year after the death of her husband in prison. She wore black mourning clothes. She seemed to him a strange woman he did not know. She stopped embracing him at night. He stopped feeling pleasure with other women. He conjured her in his imagination after her death. She was his first and last love. Her image was engraved in his heart, her voice whispering in his ear.

"What about you, what are your childhood memories?"

"I did not have a childhood."

"You're lucky."

"Why?"

"You do not have a memory full of pain to deform the pleasure of love. A man in your life is a human being, but a woman in my life is only a way of regaining an old pleasure from childhood."

"The absence of childhood means the absence of roots, like a tree suspended in the air and tossed by the winds."

"Oh! You are a student of Sigmund Freud! Childhood is not everything. The greatest creators in the world did not have a childhood. They did not have a family, no father, no mother. The creative will springs from deprivation, not from satiation. I suffer from satiation and the poverty of the spirit."

The conversation went on between them in a cruel circle, always ending with an obscure word like *spirit*. She felt that he was far from her, although he was in bed beside her, as though he were a soul without a body. Even if she reached out her hand and held him, he remained far from her. This distance made her long for him. Her desire for his body was kindled. She thought of this contradiction when she was in his arms. She wanted to live love without thinking. She wanted her mind to be severed from her body. Maybe she sought to possess him through love, or she sought to free herself from the idea of possession itself. Roustum became a necessity for her: she could not do without him, although it was necessary to do without him. Her will weakened every time they separated and broke off their relationship. She returned to him each time with increased submission and love and with increased anger and hatred for them both.

"This love is sick, my dear," Gamalat said. "Remove this Roustum from your life. Take him off just like you take off a pair of shoes. Make him a pair of shoes on your feet so he runs after you, and don't make him into a crown on top of your head, so that he bends your neck."

When she heard his voice on the phone, Gamalat's advice evaporated into thin air, like autumn leaves dispersed by the wind. The voice of Miriam the poet returned to her: "One moment of love under the light of the moon is worth a thousand years." In the mental hospital Carmen said to her, "Love is like life—it knows nothing but despair and it ends in death." Miriam objected, "Love is like life, it knows nothing but hope and it does not stop giving birth to new life." Carmen could not endure the word *birth* and said, "Women think of giving birth all the time. I mean giving birth to children. Each and every one of them fears the word *barren* like death, and a more dangerous word is *spinster*. Women run after men not out of love but out of fear, and this has no cure except—"

Carmen closed her lips in exhaustion. The young woman's eyes were fixed on her eyes. Her heart beat under her ribs. She breathed heavily as she sat beside her. The hospital was immersed in darkness and silence. The whole universe was asleep except for her, sitting in her chair, and Carmen lying in her bed. Her voice reached her as if it were coming from a distant horizon, as if she were holding her soul in her hands and was hovering with her above the city. Her lips parted with a whisper, as if she were speaking in her sleep. She feared raising her voice.

"Except what, Carmen?"

The answer came in a voice that did not resemble Carmen's prior to her admittance to the hospital, before the the electric shock treatment.

"Except writing, my daughter."

The word *daughter* rang in her ears. She heard it for the first time in Carmen's voice. Her voice had become weak and frail, like the voice of a helpless woman, a deserted wife, or a wounded mother. She was not the Carmen she knew.

The young woman was bewildered. The question circled her mind, "Does a woman's grief differ from a writer's grief?" Roustum asked her, "Does a man's grief differ from a writer's grief?"

The young woman went to Samih, who told her, "Writing lifts a man above what is called manhood and lifts a woman above what is called womanhood. Writing lifts a human being above all the differences that prevail between us."

Miriam the poet said, "Women sacrifice writing for the sake of men, for the sake of freedom and love. That is utter stupidity."

Miriam's words transported the young woman to a new horizon, as if Miriam were holding her soul in her hands, and lifting them above the clouds. Miriam drifted ahead of her over the top of the pyramids, then left her behind, lost between heaven and earth, hung in the sky like the question hanging in her head. "Did Roustum love his aunt and never love another woman?" He used to say that she was the most beautiful woman, that he had never known a woman more tender than she. He considered her tenderness a rare love, not a sin. It was a love greater than a mother's love, as she took him inside her to give birth to him in a revived form.

She was consumed by jealousy for his dead aunt. Her adversary was not a woman with a body but a ghost Roustum dreamed of at night. How could she compete with a ghost?

"You are crazy—your place is in the hospital with Carmen," Gamalat told her.

"Writing is like being crazy. It springs from the center of madness itself," Samih told her.

But Miriam the poet said, "Writing is like freedom, it springs from the center of sanity."

᷂

It was a day in August. The hot tar of the pavement was soft under her shoes. Dust rose to her nostrils with a smell of sewage and hot oil. The street, were very crowded. The faces were pale, sweaty, and heavy with sadness. Women's heads were wrapped in white, black, and multicolored scarves. The silk scarves hid stifled and angry looks as quietly as the summit hides a volcano. Eyes looked to the ground and footsteps were slow and heavy. Cars raced by, their horns honking,

173

voices from loudspeakers blaring, children shouting, and women wailing behind a coffin. The sun was directly overhead, sending down flames, and the peak humidity doubled the heat.

The young woman stopped to wipe the sweat from her face with a tissue. In that instant she glimpsed Roustum's head inside his Mercedes, his salt-and-pepper hair, his tan, and his hands on the steering wheel moving firmly and confidently. A woman with gray hair sat beside him. He looked at her and she saw a smile on his face that she had never seen before. She asked him about her when she saw him that night. After first denying it, he confessed that she had been a friend of his for years. They had a special relationship. Very special, he added.

"Roustum lives like a prisoner of the past, like me," Carmen said in a faltering voice, from her hospital bed. "I am a prisoner of the imagination whom reality fails to reach. I try through writing to bridge the gap between imagination and reality, uselessly. As soon as I finish one novel I start the next, as if writing were an attempt to free the body from the soul's grip."

"The soul?"

"I have tried to find a word other than *soul*, because old words no longer hold truth. Perhaps *spirit*. The past is dead and we try to awaken it by writing. Roustum always used to mix things up, just like me. We hide in writing so we can do what we want, live in freedom, heedless of morality."

"What is morality?"

"To be true to your word or to be faithful in love, because only love is faithful to love, and only honesty is faithful to honesty, even within the imagination."

The young woman bent her head in a long silence. She thought of the word *honesty*. All her life she had never known honesty. She loved neither Roustum nor Samih. There was another man, made of another substance, in her imagination, neither body nor soul. She avoided using the word *honesty* in her novel, maybe because she was neither a writer like Carmen nor a poet like Miriam. She did interpret God's word as Gamalat did. She couldn't conjure from her imagination a love story that had not happened. Love stories seemed to her made of the illusions of childhood.

Samih provided her with a sense of security. She went to him when illusion overwhelmed her, when her longing for Roustum became unbearable. He knew that she was not seeking him in particular, that he was not the only one in her life, and she was not the only one in his.

The sun set in the soft summer night and the young woman walked on the shore in Garden City. She saw the light in Roustum's room overlooking the Nile. She hesitated for a moment. Should she go to his house and ring the doorbell? She imagined him alone, sitting down writing or absentmindedly sipping wine. She stood at the door. Her hand rose to the bell then dropped back down. It would be best to turn around and go back to where she'd come from. Samih was at a book fair in Damascus and Carmen was at a literary conference in New York. The neighborhood seemed deserted. People had escaped to the North Coast or to the shores of Southern Europe. Gamalat spent the summer with her sister in Ras al-Bar, so the flat was hers alone. She liked to take a hot shower and stretch out in bed, filled with the pleasure of being alone. She had a desire for something mysterious. She reached for a pen. She drew faces without features and shapes without meaning.

As she sat holding the pen, the doorbell rang. Roustum came in wearing a pure white shirt. The walls of the flat seemed dark and black next to him. He had a red rose in his hand and a book with a blue cover. He had just returned from the seashore. His face was tan and his voice a little hoarse, as if he had had a lot of wine to drink and the sun had burned him and the salty seawater together.

He stuttered, then said decisively: "I have a final word for you."

The word *final* cut through her inner ear like a razor. The hall seemed narrow and the air stifled, the walls gloomy and stained. The chairs were worn out, their springs poking through the pale yellow covers. Her nightdress was creased and its sleeves torn. It displayed her poverty. She had slept in it and cried for many nights. It must smell of tears and sweat. She'd had no time to put on something else. On the table was a piece of paper with some scribbling, some amputated letters that showed her inability to write.

She became pale, sitting in her seat, as she received his final word, like a hammer blow. It hit her head once, then there was silence. She heard only the sound of the water dripping from the worn-out faucet onto the tiles in the bathroom. The sound of the loudspeakers came sharply from al-Mobtadayan Street, then heavy silence returned once more. She was sitting down and he was sitting beside her, surrounded by four walls, as if they were together inside one prison.

The hall and the flat all belonged to Gamalat. Her spirit hovered over them, from the ceiling, from the walls. The door to her bedroom was open. Her wide bed was topped with a red shiny quilt. A thick gray curtain was pulled across the window, the same color as her headscarf. Three pairs of pointed high heels stood under her bed, except one shoe with a broken heel that was turned upside down. The dressing table was near the window. On top of it was a wig, kohl, lipstick, a box of powder, an eyebrow pencil, perfume bottles, an incense stick burned down halfway, and a half-drunk cup of coffee she'd left on the table with her red lip prints on the rim.

She longed for Gamalat as she sat silently. Roustum was a stranger in this familiar place. He did not belong to her and she did not belong to him. He was from another sex, another time, maybe another planet.

For the first time she felt that Gamalat was closer to her than Roustum. They were connected by real feelings, like a mother and daughter. Roustum was no more than a specter who appeared and disappeared, feeding her nothing but fantasies.

He came close to her and held her hand. He encircled her with his arms. She left him her body, as if she were a pillow on which he could place his head and sleep. She felt nothing except that her body was something she could not possess, something made of illusions. She thought of Carmen, who was watching them from far away. She had hired a spy to follow her husband wherever he went. He watched them from a telescope in the ceiling that had a hidden lens. He was embracing her while she was thinking of Carmen. Her thoughts prevented her from experiencing the present moment. His voice was cracked, rattling and choked by tears. His words were broken.

"I finally... thought... the only solution... we break our relationship... we have held on for long... more than we should have... this is my final word... final..."

The word *final* was like a whip with which he was hitting her face again and again. She received the blows with a pain mixed with pleasure. She knew for certain that it would not be *final*, even if he repeated it a thousand times it would never be *final*, not ever. She whispered in a barely audible voice, "You play with words to get what you want."

178

He smothered her with hot kisses on her head, hair, neck, his hot lips crawling down her body. She wiped the tears from his eyes and kissed him gently like a mother. He moved away from her, smoothing his hair and his white shirt.

"I am sorry—I am crazy and you are very sane, you are too sane, you are truly a writer."

He thought, she is cold like Carmen.

It was the first time he had kissed her lips. Maybe it was shyness, like a virgin's, or fear, or something else she saw in his eyes, with her own eyes closed. His trembling fingers moved over her body. His eyes were closed but his memory was open to the past. He kissed her with the heat of childhood memory. She moved away from him as she smoothed her disheveled hair.

"Have you forgotten what you said?" Her voice was barely audible.

"What?"

"That we must end our relationship."

"Oh, of course."

He sat upright and smiled. "You should be envied for your strong memory—it's a gift that will help you write."

"Of course, we must end this relationship. We cannot betray Samih's and Carmen's trust. This is utter selfishness devoid of any conscience!"

"Conscience?"

"Yes, conscience!"

"Love does not know conscience—love is conscience itself."

"I beg you, no more playing with words."

❀

Before Carmen was admitted to the hospital she decided to finish the novel. The novel seemed to her to be free of great events like the war in Iraq, massacres in Palestine, public demonstrations in all the countries of the world, movements of resistance against war, poverty, and globalization. It was a trivial novel about the lives of individuals toying with love, wine, and betrayals. She was about to throw it into the wastebasket. Then she remembered that Roustum was deep in the midst of the election battle. It was a hot battle, resembling a battle on the killing field. The time of war for Roustum was the time of love. In his childhood, he yearned for his mother, as he shouted in the demonstrations, "No to war, no to tyranny."

❀

The young woman woke up from her sleep to the sound of a key turning in the door. Gamalat's high heels were striking the tiles in the hall. She whispered in a low voice as she entered the bath-room, "By God's name, the most merciful and beneficent. I seek refuge in God from the Devil."

She expelled the evil spirit that lived in the walls of the bathroom. She sniffed for sin in the stagnant air of the flat. She put on her plastic slippers and scuffled her feet on the floor, invoking God's name and flaring her nostrils.

"Roustum was here?"

The young woman avoided looking into her eyes. She shook her head, yes or no. They were both the same. Gamalat no longer occupied her. She had never understood her. She squatted in her bed in the winter nights with her red quilt and an ashtray full of cigarette stubs on the bedside table. She placed a cigarette between her red lips and mumbled verses from the Quran. She sipped cheap wine that stung her throat like white alcohol. She followed every sip with a puff of smoke. She thanked God for the luxuries He gave her in life and for the sins He would forgive in the afterlife. She made a place for the young woman to sit beside her in bed and told her about her dead mother and her hell-bound husband.

"My husband was a hot-tempered man. One night he heard me talking in my sleep. He kept a handgun under his pillow from the days he had been in the army. Apparently he heard me dreaming about another man. The blood boiled in his mind and he shot at me. God protected me and the shot went amiss. He told them during the investigation that he had never heard his wife moaning like that, as if she had been moaning with another man. Their blood boiled just as his had and they acquitted him. Tell me, are you writing a novel?"

"A novel?"

The young woman avoided looking into her eyes. She shook her head. She had never thought of writing a novel.

"May God curse writing and whoever invented writing," Gamalat warned. "It is easier to carry a boulder on one's back than to write. If it weren't for Bahy Boram my weekly column would not have come out. I have hated reading and writing all my life. But what can I do? God decreed that I become a big writer." Then she let out her loud and playful laugh. She was attractive to the young woman when she laughed. Her eyes shone when she spoke about love. She loved poems by al-Akkad, Shawky, and Rumi. She hummed Miriam's poetry when she was in the bathroom.

One night when the young woman was sitting beside her in bed Gamalat's hand reached out for her body. She wanted to prepare her for what she called the art of love. She encircled her with her arms and gave her a long hot kiss on the lips then she slipped her hand to her breasts and her belly and down to her private parts.

The young woman struggled to open her eyes, as if she were in a dream, or a nightmare. She heard Gamalat speaking. "Life is a brief station between sleep and death. A human being is an animal standing on two legs. What do you say, would you like to join our society?"

"What society?"

"The society for seeking the spirit world."

"Spirit?"

"And Roustum can join too."

"Impossible!"

"Why?"

The young woman did not have the courage to answer the question. Roustum had never believed in a heavenly god, so how could he believe in spirits? The word *spirit* rang in her ears, elusive, mysterious, hidden by a veil. It almost resembled Roustum's face when he brought it close to her own. His lips touched hers briefly, then withdrew, as though the kiss were in her imagination, an illusion. Nothing seemed real except the smell of his lavender cologne. It stayed in her memory along with the smell of wine. They were apart more than they were together. Each of them decided to separate from the other for good, and then they returned to one another with a force mightier than their separate wills. They never knew what it was, or where it came from. From the sky, earth, body, soul, from something that words could not name.

Roustum's voice shook when she asked him about the society. He said he was an inactive member. He would not nominate himself, or go through the ordeal of initiation. He did not believe in the spirits except as part of the imagination. In his childhood his aunt was a spirit that hovered over his bed, as if she were his absent mother or father. Her image was almost like that of God for him. He loved her and feared her at the same time. His fear won out over his love as his childhood came to an end. He stopped loving women as a young man. He was not attracted to their bodies: their plump thighs that trembled with every step did not arouse him, nor their perfumes that, no matter how strong, could not hide the smell of menstruation. Maybe he was more attracted to the bodies of young men with their muscles, their slim legs that carried no fat, and their strong and firm thighs.

Gamalat hit the table with her fist.

"I knew about this Roustum from first sight. He desires men more than women, just like Lot's people."

Then she laughed until her eyes teared and she wiped them with a tissue. "Lot's people were mentioned in the Quran by God. This proves that they are present in this world. They are fated for hellfire, my dear. Only pious men will go to the Paradise of Eden, those who are attracted to women only, and the pious women who are attracted to men only. But a man's sin is greater than a woman's sin because Lot's people were mentioned, but the lesbians were not mentioned by God, not in a single verse. So what do you think of joining our society? We have a meeting next Friday. Come with me and see for yourself, then decide at your leisure."

In a dark alley behind al-Sayyida's Mosque, in a room with a low ceiling filled with smoke, the smell of musk and incense, and a hookah that went around the group, Gamalat sat in the middle, where a circle of light fell from a hanging lamp. There were dead flies on the electrical cord and a gray straw mat was spread from wall to wall across the floor. They formed a circle and squatted on square colored pillows. A low, round table was in front of them. Bowed wooden shelves held books, magazines, yellowing papers, new Qurans with shiny covers, rosaries, incense burners, the Ramadan calendar, and a talisman for protection against envious eyes.

The group numbered twenty-three men and women. A woman in her 80s, a granddaughter of an ancient prince from the family of Mohammed Ali, an Indonesian student in his 20s who was studying law in al-Azhar, a middle-aged widow from Alexandria whose husband died in war, a former government minister from Heliopolis who had escaped with money from the country and then returned, a chemist who owned a pharmacy and worked for a medical facility, a repented, retired belly dancer suffering from breast cancer, a university professor specializing in psychiatry, a sheikh from a mosque in the al-Zamalek district, a church priest from downtown Shubra....All that had brought them together was their desire to uncover the secrets of the spirits.

Gamalat squatted on her pillow. Pain and nervousness went out of her body. Her soul was filled with peace and an aura of light shone around her. They looked at her with half-open eyes. She seemed to be a hovering spirit.

They became silent as she spoke. Her voice in the faint light seemed to be coming from another world. It was somewhat hoarse, as if it no longer came from beneath her ribs, and not from the heart, lungs, liver, or spleen. It did not belong to any bodily organ. It seemed as if it were coming from the soul.

"Only God knows about the soul. The soul is not defined by shape, content, time, or space. Our mind is unable to penetrate the body and lift the veil off the soul."

Her words were ancient, dictated by eternity. Her voice and the luster in her eyes, the way she pronounced words and arranged them one after another, together with the movement of her fingers and hands that looked as though they were playing an invisible musical instrument, made the ordinary words coming from her mouth sound extraordinary. Her voice created an ethereal sound in their heads that excited an old longing and a kind of mysterious and pleasurable numbness. All this coincided with deep inhalations from the hookah and sips of wine matured from the beginning of time. Her voice filled their heads until she stopped speaking. Childhood memories paraded before their eyes.

Roustum squatted on the pillow. He was frozen in place. He did not take his eyes off her. He was pulled by her voice and the luster in her eyes, as if she were the witch in *The Thousand and*

One Nights, or the ancient fortuneteller from whom God has lifted the veil. The image of his mother and his dead aunt returned to him, and the voice of his father reciting Quranic verses on the Birth of the Prophet.

It was the night of the Birth of the Prophet. The voice of his father, from his childhood, resembled Gamalat's. God had blessed the Prophet Mohammed in his mother's womb. She saw in a dream that a light came out of her, and the palaces in Cham were lit up and she was told that she was carrying the Master of this nation and so if he fell to the ground she should say, "I seek refuge for him in the One, from the evil of the envious." His father said that he saw in his sleep a silver chain coming out of his back that had one end in heaven and the other end on earth, one end in the East and another in the West, and then it became a tree and each leaf was made of light.

His big eyes widened like a child's as he beheld the circles of light that fell from the ceiling, the smell of incense, of burning sandalwood, and shadows of ghosts cast onto the walls, the whisperings and mutterings of holy verses, the overwhelming feeling of sin. He brought his knees together as he sat on the pillow, just as he used to gather himself like a hedgehog as a child. He felt a pleasure and fear of God and a longing for his mother. She materialized in front of him in the form of her twin sister. He became a fetus in her womb once more. She whispered in his ear, "I invoke the One against the evil of the envious. I saw in my sleep a silver chain coming out of my back that had one end in heaven and one end on earth, then it became a tree and every leaf was made of light. Roustum, you will be master of these countries. You will save them from oppression and corruption." Roustum remembered his childhood dream. He used to see himself as a prophet with whom his mother had become pregnant in obedience to God's will for the sake of saving the world. He wanted to go into the army to be trained to use weapons. He did not like killing or the sight of blood. His mind was orderly and tended toward deep thinking and reading philosophy and novels. He had been unable to save the world through philosophy or writing stories. Samih said, "You cannot save the world except through politics and elections." The way was opened for him to the Shura Council.

❧

Miriam the poet did not join the group. She was not searching for a spirit. She had an old friendship with Gamalat that went back to their childhoods. Gamalat had known deprivation, wretchedness, and rape. She was eleven years old when she gave birth to an illegitimate child. She did not look into her face, except for a quick glance, which was enough to engrave her eyes inside her. She saw them in the unconsciousness of sleep and when she walked in the streets, in any street or alley where her eyes met the eyes of a child. She did not take refuge in God and in prayer for forgiveness, but to forget. It was no use. The two eyes remained fixed in her vision, cutting her. If she drowned her mind with wine and burned her chest with smoking and stepped on her heart with her shoes, slept with women and men, laughed, roared, uninhibited, uncovered, wore the veil, did good deeds, committed atrocities, the two eyes remained in her vision as if they were part of her, as if they were her own eyes.

Miriam the poet swallowed a big tear. She hid her eyes with her hands for a long moment as if she were asleep. Her hand moved a little from exhaustion. One eye appeared wide and red, looking at the sky, steady without blinking as if it had no eyelid or eyelashes, as if her eyelid and eyelashes had been burned away by tears. It almost resembled the eye of the girl who was burned by kerosene and matches.

The trapped tear rolled down Miriam's face, who sat like a statue. Nothing of her moved, except her lips.

"Gamalat is my lifelong friend. I love her with all her madness, but she is a hustler like the palm readers or coffee cup readers, tarot or sea shell readers. She read something as a child at school about psychology and trained herself to seize upon people's weaknesses. She plays on them as if she were playing strings of a guitar. In this group she tries to break the shell of sadness, to break down the walls of fear, to free her childhood memory or her imprisoned soul."

The word *soul* rang in the young woman's ear. Her eyes widened with astonishment, as if she were waking from a long and deep sleep. The words kept ringing in her head: *her soul, her soul.* Did Miriam the poet believe in the soul?

She saw the question in her eyes and answered as if she had heard her.

"The soul is freedom. We seek freedom from birth to death. We seek freedom in love and in hate until the body reaches the height of pleasure or pain. The imprisoned knowledge inside the self is set free in the form of a long scream reaching to eternity. The scream of pleasure is not different from the scream of pain. The goal is one: to be set free from chronic bonds and chains for all eternity."

Miriam the poet gave a long sigh and she sang in the voice of someone dreaming in sleep. Her legs were stretched out on the wooden railing of the boat on the Nile.

Freedom is knowledge,
the power behind everything,
behind even poetry and novels!
Why else
is the gun in prison more innocent
than pen and paper?

The Cairo airport was almost empty just before dawn. Black clouds and thick fog obscured vision. The atmosphere was heavy with humidity, smoke, and steam. It was the middle of August. There were sounds of airplane wheels spinning onto the asphalt. The plane separated from the earth in an instant and hovered in the sky as if Samih had spread out his two arms and flown with those wings. He flew over the tops of the city's buildings, over minarets, towers, over everything. Policemen stomped on the ground with iron heels. They appeared and disappeared like shadows. The yellow newspapers filled the markets with the color of hepatitis. They increased and spread like flies. The big headlines in red ink were about the bloodshed in Palestine, Iraq, and Afghanistan, about the money smuggled out of the country, the increase in poverty and the gap between the masters and the slaves, the spread of the word *identity* in books and articles, the competition to publish the news about prostitutes and illegitimate pregnancies, the deceptions of presidents and kings in bygone eras or in faraway countries beyond the seas.

At the gate of the airport, three women wearing jalabiyas and black headscarves waited for the arrival of the dead body inside a wooden box. An old man with a curved back held the hand of a sleepy child who was blinking at what was happening around her. The young woman was standing at the exit gate staring at Samih's back as he walked, pulling a big suitcase on wheels behind him. The touch of his lips on her face at the moment of farewell was warm and soft and receded like the delicacy of air, like the receding of the soul from the body.

"Samih?"

He stood for a moment, then turned. He saw her standing at the door. Her eyes were looking at him, hard, cutting. Her lips parted with a smile. She waved to him with her upraised hand. He raised his own and waved back. His voice from the previous night passed through her ear. In his pocket was the paper on which the address was written in her handwriting, Yolanda's name, the name of the street, the number of the house, the name of the restaurant.

Yolanda invited him for a meal of *paella marinara* and Catalonian wine and kept him from being alone with the child. She feared he would flee with her to the airport. She hung onto her and spoke in Catalan and hand gestures, pointing to her heart. Samih answered her with gestures and Arabic.

"Nouria is my granddaughter. She is the daughter of my son Francisco."

"Nouria is my daughter."

"Who are you?"

"I am Samih, her father."

"How do you know you are her father?"

"She looks exactly like me. She is a copy of me."

Yolanda laughed derisively. "We do not have the word *features* in Catalonian law as features resemble one another." She uttered the word *features* with the tip of her tongue. There are forty look-alikes, as they say in Catalonia. The law here depends on scientific facts."

"You mean blood tests and DNA?"

"Yes. The tests at the lab proved that she is the daughter of Francisco."

"Science is like anything else in life, it cannot be one-hundred-percent certain. There is always something to make things less than perfect, except God, who alone is perfect."

"Do you believe in God, Samih? Here in Catalonia we believe only in science and truth."

"Truth is never final, Yolanda. Truth is relative, and there is always something missing in truth that prevents it from being perfect."

The young woman remembered this last sentence. Roustum used to say something like that about love, that there is always something missing in love to make it honest, and something missing in virtue to make it virtuous. Carmen used to say, "There is always something missing in a man to make him a man—Roustum tries to justify corruption with his relativity theory."

❦

She saw her lying in a coma in the hospital bed. They had untied the restraints from her body. Her head was hooked up to an electronic monitor and her arms were raised on top of a pillow. An IV tube carried liquid from a bottle suspended in the

193

air into her veins. Her lips were white and her chest was quiet.

"Carmen," she called softly.

Her eyelashes quivered. Her lips did not part with sound. She sat beside her at the edge of the bed in silence, as if it were forever. The present moment seemed to extend to a dead past and an absent future. She reached out her hand to touch her. She shivered, as if she had touched a dead body. The nurse came in.

"She was asking about you all the time," she whispered in her ear.

"About me?"

"Where were you?"

"In Barcelona."

"Talk to her, she might hear you."

"Is she awake?"

"Her mind is awake. Talk to her, maybe she will answer you."

The nurse handed her something as her eyes went to the door. She placed it in her hand and whispered in her ear, "Open the closet before they arrive. I was entrusted with this message. Take the novel and escape. She wanted to see you. All the time she was asking, 'Where did my daughter go?'"

It was getting dark and the hospital became a white dot in the black universe. The three men were inside a long black car that moved slowly behind a veil. It appeared like a shadow from the distance or like the Holy Ghost. The street was filled with holes and ramps that led from the asphalt to the sands of the desert.

The young woman saw them from the balcony. She stood upright like a statue with her prominent stony features. Her eyes were hard, piercing and cutting like the blade of a knife. She heard Carmen's voice whisper behind her in amputated words: "Es... es... escape... my... my... daughter... my daughter." The word *daughter* rang in her ear as she stood at the window. The light of the flashlight fell upon her head. A cell in her brain shook. One word circled, a spot of light in the dark. *Mother*.

❧

The dead body moved on the bed. Her big eyes were wide open. She saw the three men enter the room on tiptoe. The first one came forward holding a flashlight. Only the shape on top of his head was distinct, the cap of a policeman or army officer. His hand stretched in front of him holding something black and pointed. The head of the second man was wrapped in a cloth, circle after circle, the gyri of a turban, like something holy men wear. The third man was bare-headed and had a thick dark brown cigar between his lips. His long legs flexed firmly inside his tight jeans. She only saw him from behind after he came in and stood behind the young woman with his tight legs inside his jeans. He lifted his right hand and directed the black pointed thing at her back. Before she could hear the sound of a shot fired, a light fell from outside the window, exposing his compressed buttocks in the imported pair of jeans that resembled a tiger's skin. On his right buttock was a square piece of cloth made of the same material, but darker in color. It was attached to his jeans, as if it were part of them, and on it were letters stitched in red. One letter appeared after the other until the word was complete, like the advertisements on the pillars in the streets and alleys. They light up brightly then switch off, then light again from the first letter to the last until the word is complete and then it switches off again and the universe became dark.

Her mind was lit up as if for the first time before the bullet flew. Her right arm moved from the bed. Her hand reached out for the bottle that was suspended in the air above her head. She held it with her five fingers. The liquid shook inside it. It was made of transparent shiny glass. A long black tube dangled from it and ended at the needle that was stuck into her left arm. This was the last moment to save her daughter. There would be nothing after this except the void. She stole power from the talons of death. It was a supernatural power only the dying know before their last breath. Fear vanishes within death, fire, prison, hunger, madness, everything. The imprisoned soul surges with an inhuman power, as if it were divine or satanic, or both together.

With this power Carmen threw the bottle at the man. It shot out like a missile at a speed that exceeded the speed of light, then it exploded across the back of his head, causing a noise that defied the laws of sound. It woke the doctors and the nurses from sleep. It woke up patients, even those who were unconscious.

The young woman disappeared. No one chased her. The city streets and alleys swallowed her up as if she were part of them. She cut through the night with her slender and lithe body. Her features appeared to be carved out of stone. Her eyes were hard, piercing and cutting like the blade of a knife. The sky was black except for the red light at the faraway line of the horizon. The darkness lifted slowly with the first light of dawn.

When the novel was published, the earth was filled with blood and the sky was blue and serene, indifferent to what was happening on earth. The men and women who were killed were falling and their bodies got mixed together. It was impossible to distinguish the male from the female, the Muslim from the Copt, the Arab from the foreigner. Death seemed beautiful in the children's eyes because it did not make distinctions between them. The child was playing in the street when two small breasts appeared on her chest. The old man fondled her breasts before she became fully conscious, then lifted her worn dress and she was uncovered. She looked at him with her piercing eyes and his look was engraved in her memory forever. She started to know him and recognize him, even if his face changed. He did not have one face. The faces were different, related to the different parties, the high civic councils, and the free elections. His face changed from season to season. No one recognized him except her. She recognized him by his eyes and by the smell of his aftershave, more than any other mark of distinction.

The novel caused tremendous outrage. The young author had no father, no mother, no identity card. She was not well known and she was not well read. Her name did not appear on the lists of prominent female authors. Her frame was sinewy and slender, as she constantly pursued her daily bread. But her backbone was solid. The election season was near and the yellow papers multiplied like flies. The protagonist of the novel was a member of the Shura Council named Roustum. He was fifty-five years old. He seemed like an athletic man; he played golf every day. He wore an elegant suit and a black tie as a sign of mourning. He had a good reputation and was faithful to his dead wife. His face was close-shaven and he smelled of lavender cologne.

On that moonlit night, Roustum stopped in front of the kiosk at the corner of the street. The proprietor was a young man, the son of a martyr.

Prayer beads, Qurans, incense burners, Ramadan calendars, and women's headscarves were displayed at the front of the kiosk. His face filled with joy, as usual, when he saw Roustum.

"Welcome, Pasha."

The young man handed him the banned novel wrapped in a cloth, and a small piece of the substance people placed in the hookah or under the tongue.

"What is the news, Mohammed?"

"The euro is going up, Pasha, and the dollar is coming down."

Roustum handed him an envelope. The young man disappeared into a wooden vault, then returned holding a black plastic bag.

"Count them, Pasha."

"Shame on you, Mohammed."

"How many calendars do you need, Pasha?"

"There is no need, Mohammed. Success is guaranteed."

"The whole nation is with you, Pasha, and congratulations on winning the award."

"God bless you, Mohammed."

At night before he went to sleep, Roustum took the cloth off the novel as if he were taking the clothes from a woman's body. He loved reading while smoking and drinking. His desire was aroused by the forbidden. As the old adage says, Everything that is forbidden is desired.

The young woman's photo was on the cover, inside a small square. His eyes were fixed on her

199

piercing eyes, as if he had seen them before in a dream or while he was sleeping. He switched off the light beside his bed, buried his face in the pillow and cried until he fell asleep.

❦

The novel got published and caused tremendous anger. Voices shouted from loudspeakers and cars beeped their horns and police whistles blared. Men in khaki trousers spread out in the streets, fields, in cul-de-sacs, searching for the novel in libraries, shops, on the pavement on street corners, under mattresses in the houses. Everywhere except in Roustum's house. He enjoyed the privilege of protection, as a member of the Shura Council. As usual for those who hold high positions, no one asked him about anything. The higher one's position, the less responsibility one has to the law and to regulations. Responsibility increases if one is a woman, even a woman who happens to be dead.

Carmen was not dead. She lives in her novel, at least in Roustum's memory. He placed her chair at the head of the table. Carmen will not sit there, nor will any other woman. Faithfulness toward one's wife increases after her death. Tonight Roustum will hold a celebration for her novel. He will place the novel on the marble table, to be surrounded by flowers and the eyes of the male and female admirers. He will not be eaten up by feelings of jealousy. Death seems beautiful, more beautiful than life. Death destroys jealousy and all vile emotions. The heart becomes white and pure like a white, empty page.

The doorbell rang.

"Oh, what a joyous surprise!"

Joy was no longer important. Her features were stone-like and would not perish. Her eyes pierced. They almost resembled Carmen's eyes, and all dead eyes. Death gave her the awesomeness of the gods, the devils, or the hidden spirits. She came in by the back door without an appointment. She did not follow the traditions of the refined ladies in Garden City. She came in with swift and long strides. She walked across the floor with her old and dusty shoes. She looked at him without blinking. He was attracted to her by an illogical force. He told himself that it was incomprehensible, to be attracted to a young woman with an unknown name and unknown origin. Her name was not listed among the respected female writers. She lived in a cul-de-sac in al-Sayyida. She was a poor worker from the lower class. She was illegitimately pregnant by him, or by Samih, or by some man whose name was unknown. It was an illogical attraction that superseded the mind, or maybe the soul. He was attracted to her long and slender body and the familiar and strange features of her face. It was amazing with its strangeness and its familiarity. It almost looked like the face that looked at him from the mirror every day, the same face that appeared in his sleep, like Satan. The face that looked out from posters on the walls during the election seasons, whose illegitimate child was mentioned by his opponents in the Council, whispering before they adulterated the campaign with rumors to inflame the imagination of the voters. Instead of having one son, he turned out to have three or four or more, and one illegitimate daughter, with whom he met secretly in his little house in Sahari City. They drew his picture beside the statue of Ramses the Great, from which urine rushes out to drown the city. The old pharaoh used to regard himself as sacred, along with everything that emanated from him. He used to pour his sacred water into the womb of one of the harem, even if she were his sister, or daughter. Everything that the Pharaoh did became law and legislation. O Ramses the Great, how you live forever with your stony body and features engraved in stone, with your steady gaze that does not blink. O Ramses, O Narcissus, who worships himself.

The young woman came in. This was her, the same body, and the features exactly the same: the face pale from lack of vitamins, the stony and eternally sad features, and the straight back with its solid backbone. She was proud, despite her poverty and lack of prestigious background. The old thing quivered under his ribs when he saw her. It was incomprehensible, the mixture of new bodily pleasure and old guilt, of the soul's torture and the pangs of a phantom conscience. Her eyes rose with a new look of superiority, as if saturated by a lust of the mind, and what exceeds it. Nothing would satiate her, not even the height of pleasure in bed. Her mind was forever longing, elusive and lustful. Her cheap and careless clothes appeared expensive. Her equanimity was like that of a lioness who was not satisfied even by a lion. She was neither a virgin nor a woman of experience, neither female nor male: nothing changed her. Even if she were to cross the sea and be impregnated by the seed of a tree she would return unchanged, without having gotten wet by a single drop of water. Not a single tear hung on her eyelashes.

Roustum repeated in his rattling voice, "Oh, what a joyous surprise!"

They embraced in the present moment, before it slipped into the past. He held her with his two hands, as if she were a bird he feared would spread its wings and fly. He held onto her as if he were holding onto air or to a ghost. Roustum took a step, or just half a step, back. He saw himself in the mirror attached to the wall. His eyes were gray and wet with trapped tears. He had stored many tears behind his eyes. He was afraid of falling asleep, lest he cry in his dreams.

"When did you come back from Barcelona?"

"Two months ago."

"Oh, without me knowing?"

"Were you supposed to know?"

"Of course, how else should it be?"

Roustum laughed at the joke and told himself that it was improbable that she'd been in Barcelona all that time and then came back two months ago, and did not visit before tonight."

"Tonight we have a big party."

"A party?"

She told herself that it was impossible for him to throw a party three days after Carmen's death. But it did seem possible. Something in death called for celebration, something beautiful in death that closed eyes do not see, and nothing opened them but death. Roustum did not see himself in the mirror. There was another man standing inside the mirror wearing a brightly colored tie. He had taken off his black tie after three days of mourning in order to celebrate the novel. A black tie was inappropriate for a big celebration when Carmen was going to receive the prize for the novel.

"What prize?"

"An unknown prize that the papers don't write about."

"This is illogical, Roustum!"

"It is quite logical, as the papers write only about the state's prize, and this prize is not bestowed by any state."

"Then who owns it?"

"No one. I mean everyone."

Roustum was playing with words, as was his habit. Words were his game in politics, during peace and in war, in love and in hate, in everything. Roustum had been mastering the rules of this game since childhood.

"In any case, I am happy that you have returned to us."

He repeated the word *us*, and by the plural he meant himself, Carmen, and Samih. He had forgotten that Carmen was dead and Samih abroad. He forgot their absence just as he had once forgotten their presence. He repeated unconsciously, "I am happy that you have returned," as if happiness required the absence of consciousness.

"It is an improbable coincidence."

"All coincidences are improbable."

"Including our first meeting?"

"Maybe."

"And my first meeting with Carmen?"

"And with Samih and Suzy."

"And Gamalat and Miriam the poet and everyone else."

He added silently, and my coincidental entrance into my mother's womb, in a fleeting moment of love between her and my father. And also by coincidence, my son Mohammed Idris, who coincidentally carried another man's name. He whispered to himself without looking at her, "The whole of life is coincidence and death is coincidence. A good novel is a coincidence—if it weren't for the coincidental appearance of the young woman in Carmen's life, the novel would never have come about."

"Have you read the novel?"

"Yes."

"She gave us all our real names."

"Maybe."

"Except for you."

"It's not me exactly."

"How so?"

"Maybe she is a young woman who has my features."

"I wish that Carmen was here at the party."

"Carmen is here free of particulars."

"In soul at least."

"The soul is not less than the body."

She answered him with greater confidence. He was thirty years older than her but she seemed older than him now, at least in matters of the soul. The word *soul* was elusive; it could lead him to the abyss. He had only managed to save his mind with great difficulty from the spiritual society. He had almost lost himself and fallen in love with Gamalat.

"Gamalat?"

Her soul beat when she heard Gamalat's name. Her heart had been broken to see her helpless in bed. She was paralyzed on the right side. Her left side was still alive but the other side was dead. She now spoke with half a tongue, half her brain, and half her soul. Gamalat had changed completely in a couple of months. The doorbell and the telephone no longer rang. The men and women disappeared from around her, except for Miriam the poet and Samih. O Samih! Her heart broke when she heard his name. The image of him from behind as he walked through the airport pulling a suitcase on wheels came to her. The image seemed to have been engraved in her imagination since childhood, or before she was conceived in the womb. Samih had traveled to his daughter who was born on a faraway shore. He was the only one who went to her. Maybe he felt the mysterious and elusive feelings of fatherhood that were thousands of years old, or maybe the desire to have a boy or a girl who would carry the father's name and inherit the publishing house from him.

She still stood at the entrance of the house. Roustum led her into the hallway, then made room for her to walk ahead of him, according to the etiquette of Garden City. The woman always precedes the man by a step or two. Roustum watched her back as he followed her into the bedroom. She seemed older than her age from behind, as if she were suddenly becoming senile by merely entering the bedroom. What a strange thing. Maybe she had inherited the writing gene from Carmen, or caught the virus of writing that devours masculinity, femininity, and what exceeds them. That devours life from childhood to old age at once, without the intervention of youth. The hellish genes of writing eat away the body's cells and penetrate the mind's barrier, and age yields to them.

Roustum was amazed at the moment she entered the bedroom. Maybe a woman's degradation resided in bed; maybe she could not be subjugated except in sleep. The sudden bending of her solid erect back almost ripped his heart in two. He had been about to bring his mouth close to her back to cover that curve with his lips, just as he used to cover the deep wound in her belly before he kissed her lips.

Roustum was not prepared for her defeat or for losing her in the present moment. He placed all his love, effort, joy, pain, and eternal faithfulness in the present moment with or without his volition. He didn't possess anything in life except the present, for the past was dead and the future wouldn't exist. Those were Carmen's words in her novel. Oh, all these years with Carmen, thirty years, his only love story from among hundreds of stories, after all this restlessness, exhaustion, and the written and unwritten pages in summer and winter nights, Carmen lies in a grave under al-Mokatam Mountain and will not see her novel come to light, or the celebration for its prize. Carmen died alone in the hospital just like Mai Ziyadah and like all female writers, who die with or without volition.

Roustum touched her back with the tips of his fingers. He saw Carmen's spirit hovering over the bed. He waved her off like a fly. The soul seemed to be more fragile than the body. It could be expelled by a quick movement of the hand. He rejoiced over this discovery, as though he had just now gotten rid of Carmen, or at least her body, which was more important. For thirty years he had dreamed of freedom, ever since their wedding night. He had told her to take him, but she made no effort to take him the way his aunt, who was his mother's twin sister, used to do.

Roustum filled her glass with wine just as he had filled it every time they met, as if time were a series of circles connected in one chain with no division between the past, present, and future. He would invite her next Thursday for dinner just as he used to invite her to discuss novels and they would sit in the restaurant above the pyramids away from Carmen's and Samih's eyes. He used to pray to God that their eyes would disappear from existence, that a virus would eat them, or trachoma. God never responded to his prayer, for he knew the ideas that went around Roustum's head, and one of them was the idea that he does not exist in the universe.

"This wine is tasty, is it from Catalonia?"

"No, from Spain."

"Catalonia is in Spain, Roustum."

Roustum did not know that Catalonia is a province of Spain and its capital city is Barcelona. He went to the kitchen and drank a glass of water. He swallowed his anger with some water and buried his jealousy deep down, away from any woman who knew more than he did, or any man, for that matter. But his anger with women was greater and if a woman was a writer his anger doubled or even tripled. Deep in his mind lay the firm and improbable idea that a woman had less of a mind than he did and if she happened to be his wife then she had even less of a mind. All the members in the higher and lower councils shared this idea with him: the Shura Council and the People's Assembly, the Council of Ministers, the Congress, the synagogues, churches, mosques, all houses of worship, whorehouses and every house on top of the spinning earth.

He held his head in his two hands. He felt it spinning, although his body was resting in bed. Carmen used to lie beside him and then she would get up from bed to go the bathroom to take a sleeping pill from the medicine box, slip into the library to read or write or to sit alone, sad and abstracted, as if his presence with her in the same house was strange, and even stranger his presence in her bed.

When Carmen traveled he used to stretch out on the big leather couch. In her absence, he would lie on top of it with other women, or on top of the expensive Persian carpet. He wiped away the women's smells with a yellow towel, like wiping the window of a car. He erased the dark stains that were made by women's sorrows and his drops of fluid that held thousands of sperm, and the thread of sweat that ran from the base of his neck to the crack between his buttocks, along the furrows of his spine.

He knew exactly when Carmen would come back home. The leather sofa would be wiped clean and the carpet would be washed. There would be no smell of anything feminine or masculine, nothing except his shaving cream and the lavender cologne, which he sprinkled over the surfaces as if it were a purifier of sins, like white alcohol.

Only once did Carmen return without notice. She saw him stretched out on the floor on the carpet with a woman on top of him. He stood up stumbling from beneath her, apologizing and announcing that, after all, this is not marital betrayal, not according to custom, and there is no punishment for it in the law unless the act takes place in bed in the bedroom and not in the library on top of a Persian carpet on the floor. He screamed as if he were a helpless husband whose wife had suddenly returned without his knowledge.

⁓

Roustum bent before her: he placed his face in her hands. He sobbed in a stifled voice. She embraced him and remembered Gamalat, who sobbed in the same stifled voice at night. She no longer screamed or hit the table with her strong fist. Her strength had slipped away from her, together with her faith. She no longer believed in anything beyond her half-dead body. Ever since her illegitimate child had died, Gamalat had not regained her health. The young woman stroked her head and wondered how half her body could live and the other half die. Does half her soul die with half her body? She lay in bed like a statue, half made of stone and the other half made of flesh. Half her face was dead, and had taken on the color of granite, with one half-shut eye, even as the other half had a wide-open eye, a half-attentive nose, and half a crooked mouth. The room was dark except for the light from an old streetlight in the cul-de-sac. On top of it a new advertisement blinked on and off. A new loudspeaker was fixed onto the lamppost. It was three o'clock in the morning, just before voices burst forth with the call for dawn prayer, before the doors, shutters, and windows begin slamming, before male and female beggars wake up at the door of al-Sayyida Mosque, before the car wheels erupt in al-Mobtadayan Street along with the sounds of horns, whistles, children screaming and women wailing, hymns, chants, and the beating of drums.

Gamalat looked at her with one eye. She pulled the loose muscles of her mouth to say, "Welcome back, my daughter." She had started to call her *daughter*. She asked her about her daughter. She told her that she was in Barcelona with her grandmother, Yolanda. Gamalat sighed, lifting up the hand that was not dead to the side of her head that was not dead.

"Yolanda is a Christian name."

"It is a Catalan name, Gamalat."

"Where is Catalonia, my daughter?"

"In Spain."

"And who is her father?"

"Ninety percent it is Samih."

"Ninety percent?"

"Nothing is a hundred percent except for God."

"Yes, my daughter."

Gamalat sighed. The half of her chest that was not dead rose with one flat breast under the frills of her dress. She panted slightly. The window was closed and the air stifled and filled with a familiar smell, Gamalat's smell, a mixture of wine, cloves, ginger, dry tears, and old sweat mixed with musk and feminine perfumes, powder, kohl, chewing gum, hookah smoke, cigarettes, and stifled sobs.

"Come closer, my daughter, so I may kiss you."

She moved closer. She saw her face by the light coming through the cracks in the window. It was gray, the same as the veil wrapped around her hair. It had no features, no eyebrows and no eyelashes, like an empty page in an unwritten novel.

"I was afraid to die before seeing you."

The young woman was silent.

"I wanted to tell you something."

Gamalat fell silent and took a deep breath. She reached out with the hand that was not dead to hold the young woman's hand.

"Forgive me, my daughter, so I may die in peace. I had no one except you after my daughter died. O my daughter, my heart got burned with her. My dear daughter, don't ever leave your daughter. Go to her over there, or bring her over here. Don't ever leave her like I left my daughter. Can you see that envelope on top of the dressing table?"

"Yes, I can see it."

"Take it and open it. It contains a letter I have written for you with my left hand. I was afraid to die without seeing you. Thank God you have come back, my daughter."

Then Gamalat closed her left eye, and the other stony eye remained half open.

🙎

Gamalat disappeared from existence. Nothing remained of her except the letter written with her left hand on a lined sheet of paper taken from a school notebook. Her handwriting was crooked. The letters went above and under the line, like those of a child in the first year of primary school. Gamalat was used to writing with her right hand, which had died while she was still alive. She believed that the right hand was better than the left hand because Satan stood on the left side. After she became paralyzed on the right side, she started to believe that Satan stood on the right-hand side.

Miriam the poet said, "Gamalat was my lifelong friend. Her heart was made of gold and her mind was made of tin. She could have been a writer like Carmen and Mai Ziyadah, maybe bigger, had she not become ill."

"Her final illness?"

"No, no the very first illness, at the beginning of life, that infects children when they are born or before they are born, by heredity, through their ancestors."

In her room, the young woman turned on the lamp next to her bed. She sat with the letter on top of her knees and with a pillow behind her back. Gamalat left her crooked letters on the paper and something of her particular smell in the air; a strange and familiar mixture of everything and nothing, it swam with the atoms of the air like a hidden spirit. It circled around her head as she sat down and read the letter and in her ears she could hear Gamalat's voice as if it were coming from beneath the earth.

My dear daughter, let me call you daughter, because it is a beautiful word that makes my sad heart happy. Although you were absent, you were present in my imagination all the time. I had no one in this world but my friend Miriam. For me, she was a mother, father, brother, sister, male and female friend. She was the only one who stood beside me in my time of need. I wanted to leave the flat to her before dying. She objected and said, "I have a flat and I don't need another." She did not want more of anything except poetry. She is a crazy poet, my daughter. I loved her with all her madness. She has a heart of gold, but no mind. Miriam said, "Sign over the flat to your daughter." She knew that my only daughter died by fire. She said, "You have another daughter in Barcelona. She will be in need of the flat when she returns." I told Miriam, "Oh Miriam, I wish she would come back. I used to feel she was my daughter. What a strange thing." And Miriam said, "Why is it strange? It is not necessary to become pregnant and give birth to have sons and daughters. It is not necessary that our sons and daughters are made of flesh and blood. A poem might live more than flesh and blood." I listened to her while I lay in bed with half my body dead and the other half on its way to dying and I said to myself, "Maybe what Miriam is saying is the truth. Maybe after I die nothing will remain of me except my letter for you in my crooked left-handed writing. I have been writing with my right hand since I held a pen at school. I had a friend called Angel who used to write with her left hand. The teacher would beat her with the ruler so she would write with her right hand, and we laughed at Angel as she cried. After the teacher went out, Angel would write with her left hand once more and the teacher would return and beat her with the ruler on the fingers of her left hand and say to her, "You have to write with your right hand like all Muslims." The teacher was a Muslim and she used to say, "Angel is a Christian and the Christians write with their left hands, because Satan always stands on the left side." I was seven years old and Angel was my friend and I did not know what a Christian or Satan was. Miriam the poet wrote a poem about the teacher at school. She was expelled for three days and her parents were notified. What is important, my daughter, is that I have signed over the flat to you and in the bedside table's drawer, beside the bed, there is a thousand pounds. I have to pay back the loan to Samih. Oh, my daughter, you cannot imagine the pain I feel because I forced you to ask for money from Samih or Roustum. Forgive me, my daughter. I was like the blind, I couldn't see anything, and I was walking along with the herd, the slaves. Take the thousand pounds and return them to Samih and take your daughter in your arms and don't ever sacrifice her for any reason the way I sacrificed the most important thing in the world for something that does not exist.

Roustum filled her glass with wine, welcomed her back and asked about her health. She answered that she was fine. He asked her whether or not she was happy and she said she was. He asked her if there was anything she needed and she said, "I need one thing."

He became somewhat happy and the thing under his ribs secretly beat. He wished that she would say that she needed only his love, that she had missed him, that she'd returned for his sake.

But she did not say any of that. She was thinking of her daughter Nouria, on the other shore, beyond the sea. Nothing compensates for her. If she closes her eyes, she sees her crying because of her absence. If she opens her eyes, she sees her five fingers twisted around her finger with the strength of silk thread. She is only a baby, but she has a grip stronger than metal. She cannot get free of her grip, in spite of the distance and the breadth of the sea. The five fingers of the little girl are still holding her finger, the index finger, the main finger that opposes the thumb. She thought of cutting it off with a knife to eliminate the trace of those five childish fingers.

Roustum's face seemed to her long and pale, as if he were at the end of his life. His nose had become larger relative to the rest of his features. Longer, more pointed, more like a beak. His eyes were gray and bewildered. The hair of his thick eyebrows was falling out along with the hair at the peak of his forehead. His forehead had become higher. It comprised half his skull, like the skull of a president or a big writer or a member of the Shura Council or the People's Assembly. The flesh on his neck drooped and the veins protruded under his double chin. He almost resembled George Bush the father (or the son, or the Holy Ghost). Yolanda's image came back to her, making the cross on top of her chest, and Francisco's, as he stood still as a statue in the Ramblas, and Annajell and Jordi as they shouted with the crowds, "*Guerra no*, George Bush

assassí, Toni Blair *assassí*, Aznar *assassí*, murderers."
They had ousted Aznar. Zapatero came and repudiated the war and withdrew the Spanish troops from Iraq.

"Zapatero is his mother's name, Roustum."

"Unbelievable."

"It is quite believable."

He laughed as he always laughed at her naïveté. He used to tell himself, "She is a virginal and pure young woman who is not yet burdened by sins." She used to tell herself, "He is an elusive man who does not know the worth of a woman until he loses her." She also used to say, "I will make sure he loses me, so he will know what I am worth."

"Please stay here with me."

"I have to go back to her."

"Who?"

"My daughter."

"You have a daughter?"

Roustum had forgotten everything about her. She was one of many of the love stories in his life, a flame that had been kindled and then extinguished. Roustum could not imagine that something remained of the fleeting moments of any man's life. Nothing remained, not even a memory that fed itself to the imagination in sleep.

"Yes, I have a daughter."

"Where?"

"In Catalonia."

"Where is Catalonia?"

"In Spain."

"Oh, yes."

He said *oh* in the voice of someone in pain. She told herself that he must be suffering from loneliness with Carmen gone. She looked at him silently. She saw an ordinary man sitting on an ordinary leather sofa. Roustum hesitated for a long time, then came close to her. He took her in his arms, as if she had been in his arms only yesterday. She pushed him gently away.

"Have you read the novel?"

"Of course."

"It is a magnificent novel."

"For sure."

"It ends with her death in the hospital."

Roustum moved back onto the leather sofa, away from her. He remembered that Carmen had died in the hospital. One minute before she died she had killed a man, in order to save her daughter from death.

"She was her daughter?"

"At least in the novel. Or she was the daughter of her thoughts."

Roustum leaned over and filled her glass once more. His hand shook a bit. A couple drops of wine fell onto the Persian carpet. It looked like a blood-stain. He wiped it up with extreme care, as if Carmen might see the stain. He smiled, feeling sorry for himself, and said, look at an old man wiping a stain from the carpet.

The young woman was a little surprised. She wondered whether Roustum knew himself or not, and whether knowing the self was as evasive as not knowing it. He read her thoughts like an open book. She was exactly as Carmen had described her in the novel. Her eyes were piercing and they deprived him of his weapons. He knew her opinion of him. He had suffered from a chronic illness since childhood, one that was bound to the soul.

"I am sick, and you are capable of curing me."

His body was not sick, but his mind was heavy with sin. Maybe he was in need of soothing medication, some pills that inhibit the mind, those pills psychiatrists like so much.

"Your condition is grave."

"But I am Roustum."

He knew for certain that he was still Roustum with his special self, a very special self different from all other men, including Samih.

"Samih?"

He barely uttered the name, then he tried to forget it, and she too tried to forget it.

"You loved Samih?"

He did not need an answer. He knew she loved Samih and so he wished to see him dead, just as he had wished to see Carmen dead.

"You have a black heart, Roustum."

"Love makes the heart black."

"That is not true."

"You are a naïve young woman."

"And you are crazy."

Roustum laughed when he heard the word *crazy*. It seemed to him a word of praise. Even more than praise. They say that the greatest writers are crazy. He wished for his madness to equal Ernest Hemingway's, and then he would put a bullet into his head after completing his novel. Or at least equal his wife's madness, and then he could write a novel like hers. He had never written a novel like hers, despite all the novels he had written.

"Is that the problem?"

"Yes, that's the problem."

He was sitting beside her on the leather sofa. It was strange that he was still sitting down. It was strange that the leather sofa was still there, that the window was still there and that the twilight was still coming in from the window, and that it would soon be dark, and that the morning sun would rise. The sun comes through this window and leaves every day. Nothing appears in the dark except the light of the neon sign bolted onto the lamppost in the street. One letter lights up after the other and then the sign switches off, in order to begin lighting up anew, without ever stopping.

"I like to sit on this leather sofa with the bookshelves all around me," Roustum said. "I love the smell of books, just like Carmen did. Yes, the smell of books for her was more beautiful than the smell of any man. She wanted to die sitting in the library, not lying in bed."

"Tell me about Carmen."

He felt jealous. She never asked him to speak about himself. He wanted to take her in his arms and tell her about himself, from his birth to his death. He wanted to talk to her about himself until daylight, and to take her in his arms until her body disappeared.

"Tell me about Barcelona."

"A city like Cairo, ugly and beautiful, with a lot of restaurants and people eating all the time."

"Don't go back to Barcelona."

"I will go back."

"Your home is here."

"Home is where I am happy."

"I will make you happy."

He wrapped her in his arms. It seemed that he was intending to carry her to bed, away from the leather sofa, to the upper floor, to the bedroom, where complete nakedness was possible, without any fear of Carmen. Not the nakedness of love but of war. Each of them was wounded, bleeding, even if they did not feel the pain. The windows were closed and the curtains drawn. They blocked the noise from outside: the sound of airplanes, shouts of demonstrations, bombs that bring tears and blood, lions roaring in the zoo, the rattling sound of the khamsin winds, the beggars, the cries of the loudspeakers, the trumpets and police whistles, the beating of drums in weddings, and the wailings of female martyrs and the widows of the male martyrs. The windows were double-paned so they did not let in any of this noise, as if the outside world were dead and no one was alive except Roustum and the young woman in his arms.

"I love you," he whispered in her ear. "I swear to God I love you."

"Why are you swearing to God if you are telling the truth?"

Roustum moved his body away from her. He thought, she speaks like Carmen in bed. Maybe she is Carmen, or her younger sister, or her daughter. She is an exact replica of her. Her voice is almost the same voice.

"Don't bury your head in the sand, Roustum, and leave your rear end exposed. How many women have you known, and how many illegitimate children do you have?"

She has the right to say the same things that my opponents in the elections say about me, Roustum thought. But in the end, I am a man... "Nothing shames a man except his pocket."

"Enough, Roustum. You are a corrupt old man, like a rotten fruit that has fallen from the tree and has been fed upon by flies."

He did not hear what she was saying. It was merely a sentence from a novel that Carmen had written in a moment of anger. He wanted to slap at her piercing eyes that did not blink. He would cry in front of her, if he were not embarrassed and ashamed. A man like him crying in front of a young woman like her? The tears shone in his eyes despite himself. They were visible in the faint light that slipped from behind the curtains. Always something superseded his will: a trapped hot tear from his eyes surprising him in a dark room, light slipping from behind the curtains, a song reaching his ears on Mother's Day. He remembered his absent mother and her twin sister. He remembered walking on the bank of the Nile and seeing an old dog bound with a chain. The trapped tear escaped from his eye as if he were that old dog.

"I have wronged you, please forgive me," Roustum muttered in his rasping voice. "I have wronged Carmen and every woman I have ever known. I am cursed and expelled from Heaven, like Satan. I am without a mother, like Satan. If Satan had had a mother, he would not have become Satan. Oh, what hallucinations. What has Satan got to do with what I am going through—have I come to believe in Satan's existence?" He opened his eyes wide. "Everything is absurd!" he yelled.

He repeated that word in moments of failure, when Carmen left him or when he lost an election, when he received a prize for a trivial novel, when he was attracted to a woman who was not attracted to him, when he saw photos of his illegitimate son stuck on the walls of his house. He would hit at the air with his fist and yell, "Everything in this world is absurd!" He would wave his hand and his voice would rattle. "Absurd!"

He felt her looking at him from behind his own eyes. Her eyes were piercing and her features were carved in stone, as if she were dead. He tired his eyes trying to control hers. He thought of Samih. Why did she love Samih and not him? He turned around and faced her. He raised his hand high in the air to slap at her eyes. He wanted to rip open her heart with a knife and see the man inside of it. She was Carmen, for sure, or an exact replica. She was the only woman he had loved and the only woman who had not loved him.

His Mercedes crossed the streets of Cairo. The steering wheel moved on its own under his soft hands. The seat beside him was empty. He gave it a sidelong glance in amazement. It seemed as if Carmen had been sitting there just a second ago and had left as though in a dream or in a dream inside a dream that had occurred years ago. The faces in the streets appeared asleep, half dead, strangely mummified, like the butterflies he used to press inside his books at school. The people had gray circles under eyes that had escaped death, and the eyes looked at him from behind black clouds. Roustum drove his Mercedes with greater skill while sleeping. He neither sped up nor slowed down, keeping the balance he was known for in the government party. He held the middle, he didn't like the right or the left, he never walked to the end of the road, he feared the end as much as death. He examined his face in the rearview mirror. He had never liked his face, not since he first saw it in childhood. His aunt used to say that he was beautiful. Men bore grudges against him because he was attractive to women. They competed with him in the elections and in love in the same manner. Behind him, a woman who looked like Carmen was driving her small Fiat. Carmen was chasing him in life and in death. She was supposed to depart without a trace, like all people who leave, but she had left the novel behind to embitter his life, to prove to him that she was alive even in death, and that he did not exist, even if he joined the high council and received the top prizes. He was petrified despite his balance, as if he had never written a single novel, as if his books, which were taught in all the schools, had disappeared from existence. The city streets looked at him with doubled eyes, from behind drawn shades. The streets were filled with eyes, noses, and mouths. He gripped the steering wheel. The ground shook beneath the wheels. Had he gone mad or was it a real earthquake? Millions of voices cried out, shaking the earth, "Down with Roustum!" Was it a demonstration that his opponents in the council had organized against him?

He placed his head on the steering wheel. He fell asleep for a couple of seconds. He was exhausted. He was exhausted only when he failed or when he quarreled with his wife, for whatever reason. He imagined that she really was the reason for his failure. He yelled at the top of his lungs until he fell asleep. His wife was dead and he no longer had anyone to shout at. He awoke. His hands were still on the steering wheel. His wife was not a woman. She was a writer. She shouted back at him just as he shouted at her. Her voice was louder than his, so he grew quiet. Nothing made him quiet but a voice that was louder than his own. In the end he settled into her arms. She did not desire his lips. She desired something else. Another man or another woman, or maybe the desire for writing superseded all other desires. He desired her desire. He tried to write like her, but he did not like writing. He did not regret anything in his life except the writing. The white page stared at him with red eyes like those of Satan, or his father when he was little. Open, watchful eyes that did not let him out of sight. They rebuked him for any move he made, or didn't make. They rebuked him for sitting before a white page without writing a single letter. Roustum used to tell himself that maybe his father's eyes were the reason for his failure in writing. Or maybe his wife's eyes. If Carmen had been a woman and not a writer maybe he would have been successful. It was as if writing were a virus that had devoured her.

The car turned into Garden City as if it knew the way by itself. The area was still quiet, except for a huge loudspeaker that hung from the top of a tall minaret, which had suddenly sprung out of the earth. And a new shop selling hamburgers appeared at the corner of the street, with a neon sign whose letters kept switching on and off and on and off, as if forever. He sighed audibly, remembering a poem by Miriam the poet. *There is nothing that is forever, not even love.* He added, almost inaudibly, "Not even McDonald's."

◦❧◦

Roustum tossed in bed, sleepless. The bed had grown wider in her absence. This time Carmen was not going to be absent for a short time, but forever. The word *forever* caught in his throat. He could not imagine anything being *forever*. Maybe she was in the bathroom. He could almost hear her singing in the bathtub. She had never sung in that sweet voice except when she finished a novel, as if, after the intensity of orgasm, she had gone to bathe. She filled the bathtub with warm water and scrubbed her body with soap and a sponge, as if she were washing the sin of pleasure off herself.

Roustum turned the light switch on. He saw the novel on the bedside table near the lamp, with writing on it: C A R M E N, one letter engraved after another. It almost resembled the stony features of her face, as if it were her face carved into stone, her eyes piercing, unblinking.

Roustum opened the novel. He had only the final chapter left to read. The letters seemed unclear. Was the electricity becoming weaker, or was he losing his eyesight? He remembered that he was not wearing his reading glasses. He looked for them in the bedroom, in the library, in the drawers of his desk, in the small enclave at the end of the hall, in various places in the house, with no luck. His reading glasses had disappeared. Nothing upset him more than the loss of his reading glasses before going to bed.

"Where have my glasses gone?" he shouted angrily.

...

"Where are the glasses?"

...

"Of course you can't hear me, you are immersed in the novel!"

...

"Where are my glasses, woman?"

...

Carmen never answered him. She wrote.

A man asks his wife where he left his glasses, when if he had any sense at all, he'd be asking that question of himself. But a married man's mind has no sense. He thinks that his wife is responsible for his impulses, lapses, and weaknesses of memory, for his hair thinning, the loss of his glasses, car keys, for the bottle of pills for his high blood pressure or for lifting his spirits, or for the pills that strengthen the spirit or harden his sex.

Roustum forgot that his wife had died. He screamed louder. He felt a greater freedom in her absence to be angry with her. Maybe now he had more courage.

"Where are the glasses? You can hear me!"

...

"Still lost in the novel?"

...

"The novel, the novel, the novel."

Roustum would not stop repeating the word until Carmen got fed up, threw her pen to the ground and shouted, "So what? What if I am immersed in the novel? Is it a sin to be immersed in a novel? Is the novel another man?"

"If it were another man it would be better. At least he would only occupy half your mind and I could occupy the other half, fair and square."

"Oh yes, just like being fair with different wives."

Roustum was overcome by a rush of anger as he read the final chapter. Conversation took place between the couple in the same manner it once took place between him and his wife. The moment of anger passed and Roustum recovered what he had lost. He sometimes forgot and put his glasses in the refrigerator, and he would tell Carmen that genius is forgetful, occupied with more important things. He told her about the great Lessing. One day he came home and knocked at the door, having forgotten the key. His servant looked out the window, but the darkness kept him from seeing his master. Mistaking him for a visitor, he said, "Pardon me, sir, my master is not at home." So Lessing said, "All right, I will return another time," and left.

Carmen laughed every time he told this story.

There is no harm in showing interest in a husband's favorite stories like any happy wife. It does not make her an unhappy wife. She has more freedom than other women, but it is a lesser freedom than what's necessary for writing. Something is imprisoned inside her. It is not the soul, body, or mind. It is something mysterious and deep. She tries to undo its chains. It is like a giant tied up by a rope. She tries to free it by writing, uselessly, because no woman can be free while other women are bound, and the act of writing cannot be liberated in a world in which so many liberties are absent.

Roustum sighed as he read. How true. Carmen's words seemed undeniable, given her death. In the hospital, they tied her to the rails of her bed. They directed an electric current to her brain. Their target was her head and not her body, womb, or soul. Only her head, and what was inside of her head. Her brain was what they wanted to demolish with the electric current. Her crime was in the depths of her head, where the center of the brain is. Carmen was victorious over them, in the last moment before death. The colossus rushed from inside her with a mad power, enough to destroy the world. Her movement was the last before the deprivation of all movement. It is at the final moment of despair that the last movement expresses the ultimate hope and the chained word becomes the spoken one.

Roustum finished the final chapter of the novel. He sat in bed with a pillow propped behind his back. He did not want to sleep, or to be wakeful. He desired complete darkness in order to lose consciousness. He pressed the switch to turn the lights off, but there was no darkness. Light came from behind the curtains. One letter after another lit up, then switched off, then lit anew without stopping. He told himself that nothing would remain after his death except this advertisement, and that there was something worse than death: the inability to sleep. He could no longer sleep, except in complete darkness. He used to sleep every night, without effort. Maybe he was no longer the Roustum he used to be. Maybe he never was Roustum. He resembled a man called Roustum, Carmen's husband in the novel, a member of the Shura Council, the one who received the top prizes. He was not this Roustum who huddled around himself in bed and smelled of lavender cologne and another smell resembling sweat that his nose picked up for the first time.

Roustum got up to go to the bathroom. He washed his body with soap and water in the bathtub. The water clouded with a yellow that smelled of sweat. He got out of the bathtub and looked in the mirror above the sink. He saw a person standing behind him dazzling his eyes with a light in his hand. He quickly turned round, ready to defend himself. No one was there. The light of the advertisement had slipped in through the bathroom window. He turned back and looked at his face in the mirror. The shadow appeared once more behind him. A replica of himself, standing right behind him. When he turned around, he realized the deception. He reached out for his shaving brush and covered his face with shaving soap. His nose was filled with the smell of lavender. He will go to bed to sleep with his wife. He will take her by force against her will. Nothing cures insomnia except violence and heavy sweat, flowing until he drowns in it.

He lifts his face to the ceiling. It is white and shiny except for a black spot that moves stealthily. A fly or a mosquito. He is unable to sleep in the same place with a fly or a mosquito. He climbs the ladder to chase it, but it escapes and hides. He has never been able to catch flies or mosquitoes. Maybe it escaped to the bedroom. He bends down to look under the bed and behind the dresser, without any success. A battle is shaping up between him and the mosquito. He whispers to himself, "Its brain is more clever than mine." What if his competitors were to hear him at this very minute, were to see him crawl under the bed in search of a mosquito? He dismisses the thought from his head with a movement of the hand. "Why couldn't a mosquito's brain develop, if the brain of a woman has developed enough for her to become a writer?"

Roustum jumps up onto the bed like a child. A child lives inside him, even though his body is tall and heavy. He buries his face in the pillow, as if it were his mother's breast, or her twin sister's. Suddenly, he lifts his head from the pillow. An idea occurs to him that has not occurred to him before. He goes back to the bathroom. He opens the medicine box. Inside is a plastic bottle with pills. He is used to taking one pill, or half a pill, before going to sleep. He empties the whole bottle on the glass shelf. There are thirty-four tablets. Maybe there are enough, he thinks. It would be easy enough with one glass, or even half a glass of water. It is a very easy thing. You swallow them all in one gulp.

Darkness surrounds him as he moves toward the bedroom. Now everything is as it used to be. Carmen is lying in bed waiting for him. She makes room for him beside her. She wraps her arms around him.

"I swear, you are my only love," she says.

"Whoever tells the truth does not need to swear."

"The most beautiful love is the one that's mostly lies, Miriam the poet says."

She plays with baffling words and then disappears, just as she used to disappear to work on a novel. She was unable to write in his presence. His body no longer seems to exist, he is a ghost or a soul, thinking without a body, an eye watching without sight. From far away, very far away, a light comes in through the window. It switches on and off, on and off, until it switches off completely. It stays off, and does not light up again.